NIGHT AT THE MUSEUM

BATTLE OF THE SMITHSONIAN

A Junior Novelization

NIGHT AT THE MUSEUM

BATTLE OF THE SMITHSONIAN

A Junior Novelization

Written by
Michael Anthony Steele

Based on the motion picture screenplay written by
Robert Ben Garant & Thomas Lennon

BARRON'S

All inquiries should be addressed to:
Barron's Educational Series, Inc.
250 Wireless Boulevard
Hauppauge, New York 11788
www.barronseduc.com

Library of Congress Control No.: 2008055514

ISBN-13: 978-0-7641-4270-3
ISBN-10: 0-7641-4270-4

Library of Congress Cataloging-in-Publication Data

Steele, Michael Anthony.
    Night at the museum : battle of the Smithsonian / written by
Michael Anthony Steele ; based on the motion picture screenplay
written by Robert Ben Garant & Thomas Lennon.
        p. cm.
    "A junior novelization."
    ISBN-13: 978-0-7641-4270-3
    ISBN-10: 0-7641-4270-4
    I. Garant, Robert Ben, 1970–   . II. Lennon, Thomas.
III. Night at the museum 2 (Motion picture).   IV. Title.

PZ7.S8147Ni   2009
[Fic]—dc22   2008055514

CHAPTER 1

All was peaceful in the quiet little neighborhood. Crickets lightly chirped and a lone dog barked in the distance. Stars twinkled in a cloudless sky and warm light glowed from the windows of a cozy little home.

TZAAAP!

Sparks burst from a transformer on the nearby utility pole. House lights all over the neighborhood flickered in unison. Then they blinked out completely.

Darkness.

"Dad!" cried a young girl. "The power is out."

In the now *dark* cozy home, a man fumbled through the blackness. "Hang on, honey," he replied. "I'll grab a flashlight." Pain shot up the father's leg as he banged his shin against the coffee table.

"What if this was your house?" asked a man's voice. "The power is out. Lights are dead. Your little ones in the bunk bed down the hall are crying out, 'Mommy! Daddy! Come quick, I'm scared!'"

The father raced down a dimly lit hallway. He rifled through kitchen drawers and cabinets. He frantically searched everywhere.

"You need to get there fast. You'll need a weapon," the man's voice continued. "But *first,* you'll need a flashlight. How are you going to find it in the dark? I'll tell you how...."

As the father continued his search, from out of nowhere a glowing flashlight was thrust toward him. The father's face lit with joy.

"The Glow-in-the-Dark Flashlight," said the man, offering the flashlight.

The lights in the kitchen came on and the father walked away. The power wasn't out at all. The neighborhood, the house, the father, and the daughter weren't even real. The entire event was a television commercial.

"That's right, folks," said the commercial's narrator and flashlight bearer. "I'm Larry Daley of Daley Devices." He strolled out of the kitchen set and into the main part of the studio. He moved past studio lights and television cameras.

Larry was in his early forties, had short brown hair, and wore a dark suit and tie. He smiled. "We're going to spend this next paid-programming block rocking your world!" He walked in front of a studio audience to a table covered in flashlights. "And I brought along a friend to do it. The two-time heavyweight boxing champion of the world!"

The audience applauded as the champ entered the studio. The husky bald man pointed to Larry. "Isn't he fantastic, America?" The audience clapped louder.

Larry shook the man's beefy hand. "Good to see you, Champ."

The champ pretended to throw slow punches at Larry. Larry laughed as he defended himself with the flashlight. "Whoa!" said Larry. "It works for self-defense, too!" He blocked the blows as if using a sword.

The champ gave Larry a playful shove. "That it does," he said. "But seriously, is it true that only two years ago you were a night guard at some dusty museum?"

Larry nodded. "It's true, World Heavyweight Champion of the World," he said, playing to the audience. "I was just a regular Joe with a flashlight and a dream."

The champed nudged him. "Don't you mean a regular *Larry?*"

Larry chuckled and rolled his eyes. "Leave the jokes to me, Champ."

The former boxer laughed. "And a comedian, too." He pointed to the audience. "But I'll tell you what's *no* joke....Larry here is the founder of Daley Devices, creator of such indispensable items as the Super Big Dog Bone, the Unlosable Key Ring...." He grabbed a flashlight from the table and held it up. "Say it with me, America..."

The audience joined in and shouted, "The Glow-in-the-Dark Flashlight!"

That's my favorite part, Larry thought.

He stood in the large reception area of Daley Devices, watching the commercial on the huge flat-screen monitor. Larry chuckled and went back to typing on his personal digital assistant. Keeping his eyes on his PDA, he nodded politely at a few passing employees.

It was true that he used to be a museum night guard. It was there that Larry came up with Daley Devices' best-selling products. Most would think working the night shift at a museum would be the perfect place for a young inventor. There would be plenty of peace and quiet to think of new ideas. However, the Museum of Natural History was anything but quiet at night.

Before the museum, Larry had no direction in life. He would lose job after job while working on all kinds of get-rich-quick schemes. He never put much effort into either and always failed at both. While taking charge in the museum, Larry learned to take charge of his life. Now he was a successful entrepreneur and businessman. He was doing what he always wanted to do. Or so he thought.

Larry continued to scroll through files on his PDA when Ed joined him. The energetic young man was Larry's personal *human* assistant.

"Great news, Larry." Ed beamed. "The big meeting is all set up!"

Larry didn't look up. "When?"

"In three days," Ed replied.

"Okay," said Larry. "We have a lot of work to do."

Ed shook his head. "And we *will* do it. But can't we just be happy for a second?"

Larry grimaced. "I don't have a second, Ed." Then Larry's PDA beeped. He read the new e-mail. "You see that? That was our competitor outselling us by a hundred thousand units. Because we wasted a second talking about being happy."

Larry scrolled through his calendar as they left the building. The two men stepped out onto the busy New York sidewalk. A black sedan was parked at the curb. An older man in a dark suit stood patiently beside it. Upon their appearance, the chauffeur opened the rear door.

Larry turned back to Ed. "Go ahead and cancel my lunches and clear out your evenings," he ordered. "We're going to be working right until we sit down at that meeting."

Larry didn't wait for a reply. He ducked into the sedan and the driver shut the door. Larry buried his face once more into his PDA. His fingers flew over the tiny keys as he replied to e-mail.

When the driver got behind the wheel, he glanced back. "To the museum, Mr. Daley?"

"What's that, Denny?" Larry asked.

"It's the first of the month," his chauffeur reminded.

Larry looked up. "Right, that's today." He glanced at the plastic bag on the seat next to him. It came from a local pet store. Denny had thought of everything. Larry smiled and put away his PDA. "Yes, we're going to the museum."

Once a month, Larry visited his former place of employment. He would spend the night among all the exhibits he used to guard. Unfortunately, Larry had been very busy lately. It had been several months since he had a chance to stop by.

A short time later, the car pulled up to the Museum of Natural History. "Thanks, Denny," he said, opening his own door. He grabbed the plastic bag and stepped onto the curb. Looking back, he smiled at his driver. "You can go home. I'm going to be late."

As the car drove away, Larry began climbing the steps. The enormous stone building towered over him. The warm light from the setting sun washed over the grand columns and tall center archway. Large banners hung on each side. They showed images of dinosaur skulls and ancient Egyptian art. There was also a new banner stretched across the museum. It read: Closed for Renovations.

Larry made the last few steps and darted toward the revolving doors. He knocked on the glass. After a few moments, a familiar face came into view. It was Dr. McPhee, the museum's director. As always, the short man was perfectly groomed in his sharply pressed three-piece suit.

"Excuse me, civilian," McPhee said in a British accent. He waved his hands in a shooing motion. "Don't you know how to read?" He pointed up at the banner. "The museum is closed for..." His eyes widened in recognition. "Oh, it's you."

The director turned a latch and Larry pushed through the revolving doors.

"Why if it isn't our very own Mr. Success Story," said Dr. McPhee. He rolled his eyes. "Mr.

I'm-Too-Good-For-Eleven-Fifty-An-Hour." He laughed at his own joke. "Come for another one of your nostalgia tours? We haven't seen you in a few months."

"Yeah, I've been busy," said Larry.

From the looks of things, the people at the museum had been busy, too. The huge lobby was much different than Larry remembered. Usually, the marble floors were clear around the large *Tyrannosaurus rex* skeleton that greeted visitors. Now, the open space was filled with clutter and activity. Workers were busy hauling large crates on handcarts. They stacked them near a growing pile in the center of the large room.

"What's going on here?" asked Larry.

Dr. McPhee grinned. "Progress, Mr. Daley. The future!"

He led Larry toward the Teddy Roosevelt exhibit. The wax figure sat motionless atop his horse. McPhee gestured toward a large, stainless-steel octagonal disk on the floor. Larry had never seen it before. He reached down and flipped a switch on the device. "Behold! Natural History version 2.0!"

Larry flinched as a beam of light burst from the mechanism. However, the light quickly focused to become a small version of the museum building. The octagonal device was a hologram projector. It made three-dimensional objects out of light.

Larry stepped forward as the museum image morphed into a cloud of static. Then it transformed into a hologram of Teddy Roosevelt riding his horse. The small figure grew larger as the horse ran in from the distance. The horse and rider came to a stop when they were almost the size of the wax versions behind them.

The hologram of the former president smiled. "Welcome to the Museum of Natural History," he said, "where history comes to life." The hologram gave a wide grin. "Where should our adventure go today?" He pointed to Larry. "You there! What's your name, pilgrim?"

"Uh, Larry. Larry Daley."

"Well it's a delight to meet you"—the hologram paused—"Larry, Larry Daley." He motioned for Larry to move forward. "Step up and ask your question. Then give the next little boy or girl a turn."

Larry glanced back at McPhee. The director smiled and nodded. Larry stepped closer to the projected president. "Uh, okay. Where were you born?"

"Right here in New York City," replied the hologram. "Twentieth Street. In the year..." He suddenly disappeared.

"Blah, blah, blah," said McPhee, his finger on the power switch. "History...learning...changing America one child at a time."

Larry was impressed. "So you guys are adding some new interactive exhibits."

McPhee shook his head. "Nothing gets past you, does it, Mr. Daley?" He gestured to the large metal disks scattered about the lobby. "Yes, they'll be *replacing* the old exhibits, effective immediately."

"Wait, what?" asked Larry. "Where are the old ones going?"

McPhee waved his hands. "Away. Look around, Mr. Daley."

Larry gazed at the pile of nearby crates. He realized what was inside. They were all the old exhibits.

"We're getting rid of all this junk," continued McPhee. "The dioramas, the wax figures, even some of the shabbier old animals." He reached into a small crate and pulled out a frozen monkey. "Such as this ratty little monkey."

The director turned and casually tossed the monkey backward, missing the crate. Larry dove forward, catching the primate just before it hit the ground. "Actually, he's a capuchin," Larry corrected. He gently placed the monkey into the packing straw.

McPhee frowned. "No, Mr. Smarty Pants, he's rubbish." He slammed the crate's lid.

"Who decided this?" asked Larry.

"Myself, of course," McPhee replied. "And the board of directors. Well, mainly the board. Why do you look so perturbed?"

"I'm just...these guys *are* the museum." Larry glanced around. "People love these displays."

"People, Mr. Daley, love what's next," the director explained. "You should know that better than anyone. *You* left."

"I didn't leave, okay," said Larry. He felt a little embarrassed. "I just...my business started taking off and...my situation changed."

McPhee placed a hand on Larry's shoulder. "You don't have to justify yourself to me. You became a success. If I were a night guard, I would have to kill myself. I would literally end my life. In fact, right now, at this very moment, I'm getting depressed just thinking of being a night guard." He shuddered. "Do you have any idea about the revolving door of crazies I've had to hire to replace you?" He waved his arms about, pretending to be one of the guards. "Oh, Dr. McPhee, I can't handle this job. The T-rex comes alive every night!"

"Uh, yeah, that *is* crazy," said Larry. He pointed to the crates. "So where are these guys going?"

"Deep storage," replied McPhee. "The National Archives."

"Where's that?" asked Larry.

"Washington, D.C. Underneath the Smithsonian," the director replied. He grabbed an overcoat and scarf from a nearby crate. He marched toward the front door.

"Wait," said Larry. He hurried to catch up with McPhee. "Maybe I can talk to the board or something?"

The director laughed. "Oh yes, that would be quite entertaining. Buy me a ticket to that sidesplitting matinee." He jutted out his lower lip, mocking Larry. "Hi, could you please not get rid of these dusty old wax exhibits?" Then he straightened, imitating a board member. "Of course we will, Larry, our former night guard who doesn't know anything about anything except...night guarding." McPhee laughed at his own performance.

"But there has to be something I can do," said Larry.

The director slapped him on the shoulder. "Yes, well, not really. They're leaving in the morning." He threw the scarf around his neck and pushed through the door. "Cheerio."

The workers finished packing up and went home for the night. Just like his old job, Larry was alone in the museum. He plopped down on the base of the T-rex exhibit and buried his face in his hands. He didn't know what to do. There had to be some way of convincing the board to keep the exhibits. As Larry sat deep in thought, he didn't realize what time it was. The light faded from the large arched windows as the sun set.

Ever so quietly, the giant skeleton above Larry began to move. Long talons scraped against the stone base as its feet flexed. The huge skull turned and stared at Larry through empty eye sockets. Its mouth opened, exposing rows of large sharp teeth. Its bony neck extended as it lowered its head toward the former night guard.

Larry could feel hot breath on the back of his neck. He looked up and found himself face-to-face with the huge dinosaur skull. They stared at each other for a moment.

Then Larry smiled. "Hey, boy." He rubbed a hand over the beast's hard snout. The huge skeleton wagged its long bony tail. It nuzzled Larry and almost knocked him off the base. Larry laughed. "Yeah, good to see you, too, pal. How are you doing?" He pointed to the shipping crates. "You okay with all this?"

The huge dinosaur didn't seem to care about the boxes. He shoved his nose toward the bag from the pet store. Even though he didn't have lungs, Rexy was somehow able to sniff the plastic bag.

"What? You think I have something in here for you?" asked Larry. "Do you, boy?"

The dinosaur's tail wagged faster as Larry pulled out a long knotted rope. It was the kind of large toy made for a Great Dane or a Saint Bernard. However, Larry kept pulling to reveal several of the dog toys tied together.

The dinosaur snatched up one end of the long rope. Larry quickly grabbed the other. "You think you're stronger than me, Rexy?" He planted his feet as the T-rex tried to pull it away. "Yeah, I don't think so." The bony tail wagged faster as the two played tug-of-war. Larry's shoes slid across the marble floor. The large dinosaur easily pulled him through the lobby of the special museum.

The Museum of Natural History was very special indeed. It contained a mummy named Ahkmenrah and his one-of-a-kind gold tablet, the Tablet of Ahkmenrah. It was a magical tablet that made every display in the museum come to life each night. Only Larry, his son, Nick, and a few others knew the secret.

Larry had created his great inventions to help him deal with exhibits that came to life. Thanks to a mischievous capuchin monkey named Dexter, Larry invented the Unlosable Key Ring. Each night, Dexter tried to steal Larry's ring of keys. And if Larry didn't have his keys, he couldn't lock up some of the more *unruly* exhibits. If Larry didn't lock up the lions in the Hall of African Mammals, they might try to eat him!

The Super Big Dog Bone sprang from the need to keep the giant *Tyrannosaurus rex* skeleton occupied. Oddly enough, Rexy enjoyed playing fetch with one of his fossilized rib bones. Larry ended up tying the bone to a toy car to keep the huge dinosaur out of his hair. Rexy would follow the car throughout the entire museum.

Larry owed a lot to the museum and many of its exhibits. Dealing with the mayhem that ensued each night taught him how to put his own life in order.

Rexy shook his head, whipping the rope playfully. Still holding on to the other end, Larry flew off the ground. He lost his grip and went soaring across the lobby. He slammed against the hard floor and slid to a stop in front of the crates. As he got to his feet, he looked up to see the wax figure of Teddy Roosevelt. The twenty-sixth president was no longer lifeless and stiff.

"Lawrence!" said Teddy. "Good to see you, lad!"

"Yeah, you, too, Teddy," said Larry. "Look, McPhee just told me what's going on around here. I had no idea."

Teddy nodded gravely. "Indeed. Much has transpired since your last visit, Lawrence."

The nearby crates thudded as the rest of the exhibits came to life. Attila the Hun was king and general of the Hun Empire. He created one of the most dreaded armies Asia had ever known. The wax mannequin of the ruthless conqueror climbed out of a shipping container along with three of his warriors. They sneered in disgust as they dusted foam packing peanuts from their leather armor.

A curious Neanderthal poked his head out from the side of another crate and looked around. Seeing it was safe, the hairy caveman slowly emerged. Two others followed him. The last one looked around as he snacked on a handful of packing peanuts.

The lid from a long crate creaked open. A beautiful Native American girl lay inside. She had black hair worn in two long braids and was dressed in a beaded buckskin skirt. She was Sacajawea, the Shoshone scout for Lewis and

Clark's expedition across early America. She pushed off the lid and sat up.

Larry's PDA buzzed. "I'm sorry, just a second," he told Teddy as he checked an incoming message.

A tiny knocking sound drew Larry's attention. A lid on a smaller wooden crate was open only half an inch. "Hey, Johnny Crackberry," yelled a tiny voice. A little gloved hand reached through the crack. "Want to lend a hand over here?"

Larry leaned in. "Oh hey, Jed. How are you doing?" He pried off the top and the tiny cowboy climbed out. He was followed by Octavius, a tiny Roman commander.

The museum contained a special diorama room where several miniature displays depicted life in different time periods. One Roman display showed columns of soldiers marching in front of a miniature coliseum. A Mayan diorama depicted the life around a grand Mayan pyramid. Jedediah was a miniature cowboy from a Wild West diorama. Octavius was from the Roman display.

The little cowboy sat on the lip of the crate with his boots dangling. He peered up at Larry. "Well, lookee here! Mr. Big-in-the-Britches himself! Come by just in time to see us off."

"Yeah, Jed, I just heard," said Larry. "I don't know how this happened." Then Larry's PDA buzzed again.

"Gee, I wonder how it happened," Jedediah said sarcastically. "Maybe the answer's on the magic buzzing box. You weren't here, Gigantor," Jedediah continued. "That's how it happened."

Larry put the PDA away. The small cowboy had nicknamed Larry *Gigantor* early on. Larry didn't like the name at first, but he quickly grew used to it.

Octavius paced along the lip of the crate. He held his tufted helmet under one arm. "The truth is, Larry, there's no one else to speak for us during business hours."

"None-none, Dum-dum," boomed a loud voice. It came from the huge stone Easter Island head in the corner.

Larry noticed that *all* the exhibits were looking at him. "Look, guys, I'll call the board first thing tomorrow. I have some pull now. I'll handle it. We're going to be okay here."

"We?" asked Jedediah. "Wake up, Gigantor! There ain't been a *we* in darn near two years!"

"What's done is done, Larry," Octavius added. He gazed at the rest of the exhibits. "Even the glory of Rome had to come to an end."

"Look, guys, maybe it won't be so bad," said Larry.

Attila the Hun marched forward. "*Mooska lavootee! Koska mitoo!*" he barked.

"Just hear me out, A-man," said Larry. He addressed everyone. "We're talking about the Smithsonian here. That's like...the big leagues. It's the hall of fame of museums."

"That ain't the point, Gigantor," said Jedediah. "The point is we're being shipped out! This Smithsonian could be the Shangri-doodle-la. It ain't never going to be home."

"Forgive them, Lawrence." Teddy patted him on the back. "It's an emotional time for all of us." He turned to the others. "It's also our last night as a family. And I won't see it squandered. So who will join me for one last stroll within these hallowed walls?"

The rest of the group nodded and slowly dispersed. Some roamed the lower corridors. Others slowly marched up the marble steps to the second floor.

Teddy reached a hand down to Sacajawea. "My dear? Shall we?" He helped her onto the back of his horse. She wrapped her arms around his waist and rested her head on his shoulder. They slowly rode toward the interior of the museum, following the others.

For the rest of the evening, Larry didn't have the good time he envisioned. Since he quit being a night guard, his monthly visits were more fun. Most of the time, he would even bring his son, Nick, along. Tonight, he was glad he didn't. The evening passed in nothing more than solemn small talk.

The museum windows brightened as dawn approached. The exhibits slowly made their way back to their crates. Larry said his good-byes as the Huns and Neanderthals climbed back into their shipping containers. The cowboys and Romans from the diorama room filed back into their crates like lines of ants.

Teddy and Sacajawea rode back into the lobby and climbed off the horse. The former president held her hand as she gingerly stepped into her crate. As she lay down in the box, he

leaned in and kissed her softly on the cheek.
"Travel safe, my love." She reached up and
gently wiped the tear from his cheek.

Larry gave the couple some privacy as he
turned to the rest of the departing exhibits. He
saw Dexter busily rearrange the straw in his
box. "Hey, Dex," said Larry. "You want some
help there?" The monkey glared at Larry and
shook his head. "No?" asked Larry. "You sure?"
Dexter gave an angry screech. Then he reached
up and slammed the crate lid, sealing himself
inside.

Once Sacajawea was settled, Teddy climbed
back onto his horse. He wiped his glasses, then
rode over to his pedestal. Larry followed.
"Where's *your* crate, Teddy?"

"I won't be making the journey, Lawrence,"
he said with a weak smile. "It seems that I, Rexy,
and a few other signature items will be staying.
For now."

"Without the tablet?" asked Larry.

Teddy glanced around then leaned forward.
He spoke in a whisper. "In truth, Ahkmenrah's
tablet will be staying with him upstairs."

"What?" asked Larry.

Teddy nodded. "They're going without the tablet, my friend. I'm afraid this night was their last."

Larry watched as all his friends finished packing themselves up. After they were away from the tablet, they wouldn't come to life ever again. "They don't know?" asked Larry. "You didn't tell them?"

"There are times, Lawrence, when it is more noble to tell a small lie than to deliver a painful truth," Teddy whispered. He turned and smiled at Sacajawea. His eyes filled with tears as she closed the lid on her crate.

"Are you going to be okay?" asked Larry.

Teddy sat straight in the saddle. "I shall do my best. And who knows? Sometimes, the greatest change carries with it even greater opportunity." He put his hands on his hips. "Look at you, Lawrence. You left this place and made quite a life for yourself."

Larry couldn't take his eyes off the crates. "Yeah, I guess so."

"Well, I should hope you would do more than guess, my friend," said Teddy. "Captain of industry. World at your fingertips. Seems to me you have everything you ever wanted."

Larry straightened up. "Yeah, no...things are...great."

Teddy smiled. "If I may, lad, allow me to share with you one piece of advice." He pulled his saber from its scabbard. He leaned forward and held it high. "The key to happiness...to *true* happiness is..."

Larry's PDA buzzed. "I'm so sorry. Just hang on a sec." Larry scanned the message, then put the device away. "All right, sorry," he looked back up at Teddy. "Key to happiness..."

Just then, sunlight poured through the museum's arched windows. Teddy and all the other exhibits became frozen in place.

Larry wouldn't hear the rest of Teddy's advice. "Oh, come on!" he shouted.

CHAPTER 2

"So they're gone?" Nick asked. "There's nothing you can do?" He opened the door to Larry's apartment.

"I wish there was," said Larry. With the armload of bags, he followed his eleven-year-old son inside. "I spoke to McPhee. I called the board. But the exhibits shipped out this morning."

With a free elbow, Larry flicked the light switch. His luxury apartment came into view. It was furnished with contemporary furniture and had an amazing view of the city. It was much nicer than the many dumps from which he had often been evicted.

He set the bags onto the kitchen table. Nick watched him in amazement as he pulled out box after box of Chinese food.

"Dad, this is a lot of food," said Nick.

Larry winced. "Uh, Ed from work is joining us later. There are a couple things that we have to go over."

Nick sighed. "You're working tonight."

Larry tussled the kid's short brown hair. "Yeah, what's the big deal, buddy? I used to work every night."

Nick rolled his eyes. "That was different. That was when you had the coolest job in the world."

"Yeah, well cool doesn't pay for your school or this apartment," Larry explained. "Besides, my job is just a different kind of cool."

Larry pulled out the last of the boxes when the phone rang. He hit a button, turning on the speakerphone. "Larry Daley," he answered.

"Gigantor!" said the voice from the phone. "It's me, Jed!"

Larry's mouth fell open. "Jed? What? How did you dial?"

"Long story," Jedediah replied. "Listen, the monkey stole the tablet and now we're in a world of hurt!"

"Wait, slow down." Larry shook his head. He and Nick crowded near the phone. "What are you talking about?"

"Kahmunrah!" shouted Jedediah.

"Who?" asked Larry.

"I don't know! That's what he said his name was," Jed replied. "He's Ahkmenrah's big brother." There was the sound of a struggle in the background. "He's here, and trust me, he's not a friendly!" Someone in the background screamed. There was the sound of metal clashing. "I don't know how much longer we can fight them off," Jed continued.

"*Calla Foota!*" yelled another voice. It was Attila.

"Jed! Listen to me," said Larry. "Just hang in there!"

The sounds of battle grew louder. "What did you say, Gigantor?" asked Jed. "Hey...HEY!" The line went dead.

"Jed!" yelled Larry. "Jed?"

Only silence.

"Grab your jacket," he told Nick. "I'm dropping you off at your mom's."

"What are you going to do?" Nick asked.

"I don't know," replied Larry. "But you heard Jed. They're in trouble. I've got to get down there."

They rushed out of the apartment and headed for the elevator. As the doors opened, Ed emerged. His arms were full of notebooks and stacks of paper.

"Larry! Hey, where are you going?" asked Ed. "I thought we were working tonight."

"Something's come up," said Larry. "I have to head out of town."

Ed blocked their path, his eyes wide. "Whoa-whoa-whoa! Wait-wait-wait! Hold on a second. You *do* understand that the big meeting is the day after tomorrow, don't you? This is the one we've been waiting for!"

With Nick in tow, Larry pushed past him. "And I'll be there, Ed. But right now, I have to go." He and Nicky stepped into the elevator. Larry pushed the button.

"Where are you going?" asked Ed.

"Washington," replied Larry. Then the doors closed.

After dropping Nick off at his mother's apartment, Larry caught a cab to the airport.

Between overbooked and delayed flights, Larry didn't get to Washington D.C. until the next day. By the time his plane landed and he took a taxi to the Smithsonian Museums, it was late afternoon.

The Smithsonian was sectioned off into several buildings surrounding the National Mall. The long grassy park between them stretched from the domed Capitol building to the tall Washington Monument.

The taxi dropped Larry off at the Air and Space Museum. The huge building was built like an enormous hanger and housed aircraft of all kinds. There was everything from fighter planes from World War I and II to the first airplane built by the Wright brothers. Rockets and helicopters were scattered across the floor while planes from every era were suspended from the ceiling. High catwalks spanned the museum, giving people a chance to inspect the dangling craft. There was even a life-sized diorama of the moon landing. It was complete with wax statues of astronauts.

Larry happened upon a group preparing to tour the museum. The tour guide, a young girl in a red jacket, smiled at the small crowd.

"The Smithsonian comprises eighteen different museums. Air and Space is just one of them." She pointed to the aircraft around her. "How about all these planes? Trippy, huh? Come along, folks, we have a lot of ground to cover."

Larry pushed through the crowd as they began to move out. "Uh, hi, excuse me? Can you tell me how to get to the National Archives?"

The girl stopped and smiled. "Uh, sure. Be a historical artifact worthy of storing for all eternity." She gave a blank stare then broke into a smile. "I'm just kidding. The archives are underground in a secure area," she explained to everyone, not just Larry. "They're not open to the public. It's too bad, too, because I saw them once and, gang...it's a trip."

Larry let the group continue without him. He made his way through the large museum, looking for any way to access the archives below. He passed a monkey in a space suit that bore a striking resemblance to Dexter. He wove through more historical aircraft. He even passed a gift shop where dozens of Albert Einstein paperweights bobbed their tiny heads as he went by. The museum was filled with many wonderful things but he blew by them all. He had to get to his friends.

Not finding what he needed, he left the Air and Space Museum and made his way toward the Castle. The oldest of all the Smithsonian buildings, the Castle was aptly named. Gothic towers and medieval-styled parapets adorned its roof. Its scarlet stones made it stand out among the pale marble structures surrounding the National Mall.

Larry looked at his watch, then glanced toward the Washington Monument. The sun seemed to teeter on the point of the tall stone structure. It wouldn't be long before sunset.

Oh, man, Larry thought. *I'm running out of time.*

Once inside the Castle, he found himself in a large vaulted atrium. Light streamed in through a giant stained-glass window at one end. The huge area was dotted with large display cases, information kiosks, and freestanding exhibits. Several smaller galleries branched off from the main hall and flowed through the rest of the building.

He passed a large exhibit dedicated to the American gangster. A couple of well-dressed mannequins holding tommy-guns stood by several video monitors and photographs. The monitors ran loops of old gangster movies while the photographs showed various shots of Al Capone, the most infamous gangster of all. A life-sized, black-and-white cardboard cutout of a young Capone held a devious smile.

As Larry continued his search, another display caught his eye. It was a freestanding stone wall covered with Egyptian hieroglyphics. The large marble door in the center was adorned with a carving of a screaming skull. Something about the ominous exhibit gave Larry pause. He moved in for a closer look. Beside the wall stood an information plaque on a pedestal.

The Gate of Kahmunrah—Mythic Door to the Underworld.

"Kahmunrah," Larry mumbled. That was the name Jed mentioned over the phone.

Larry looked up from the plaque and his eyes widened. A familiar shape was carved into the door. The indentation was the exact size and shape of the Tablet of Ahkmenrah. Larry leaned even closer.

"Hey!" barked a voice beside him.

Larry looked up to see a security guard glaring at him. The young man had short greasy hair and braces on his teeth. His dark blue uniform looked as if it hadn't seen an iron since it was first issued.

The guard grimaced. "No touching!"

Larry backed away from the display. "Oh, I wasn't going to…"

"Really?" interrupted the guard. "Because it looked to me like you were moving in with I-T-T." He stepped forward. "Intent to touch."

Larry shook his head but the guard continued.

"If you want to, go right ahead. Touch it," he said. "I stand around all day just waiting for some punk like you to come along and make my shift interesting."

Larry couldn't believe it. Of all the people for a gung-ho security guard to go after. "Are you threatening me?" Larry asked. Then he glanced at the kid's name tag. "Brandon."

"I don't know, Princess." Brandon smirked. "Am I?" He slowly pulled open the right side of his blazer. Instead of revealing a sidearm, a long black flashlight hung from a loop on his belt.

Larry leaned forward for a better look. He recognized the brand instantly. "Quik-Beam, nine volt?" he chuckled. "Interesting choice."

"What are you talking about?" asked Brandon. He looked hurt.

"The hardware," replied Larry. He pointed to the kid's flashlight. "I was always more of a Biglite 65 guy. But to each his own, I guess."

The two stared each other down—museum guard to former museum guard. Then Larry noticed a security key card clipped to the kid's lapel. When he finally found an entrance to the archives, he might need a card like that to get in. Larry had an idea.

"Okay, I'll be going now," he said, breaking the tension. He crossed his arms behind his back. He pretended to be disinterested and walked away. Then he slowly circled back toward the wall. He locked eyes with Brandon as he stopped. Larry's eyes narrowed as he reached out a hand. He raised an eyebrow, extended one finger, and...*touched* the exhibit.

A grin spread across Brandon's face. "Oh, now we're going to dance, tough guy." He marched forward, whipping out his flashlight. "I had you profiled from Jump Street. I *knew* you were a toucher!"

As Brandon lunged for him, Larry sidestepped. In a fluid motion, he twisted the guard's flashlight hand and spun it behind his back. Larry wrapped his other arm around the kid's chest while he wrenched the flashlight free. He held the guard tight, shoving the light under the kid's chin. He leaned in close, his mouth next to Brandon's ear.

"Seriously, you don't know who you're dealing with," he whispered. "You think you know what it means to be a museum guard? Trust me, you don't know the meaning of the word." Brandon struggled but Larry held tight. "I've seen things you can't imagine. So let's just dial it down a notch. I'm going to let you go, and we're going to go our separate ways, understood?"

After a brief pause, Brandon nodded and Larry gradually let go of his arm. Quivering, the guard took a step back. Larry raised the flashlight and Brandon jumped when Larry popped open the battery compartment. Four large batteries slid out and hit the floor. Then Larry tossed the empty light toward him. "Watch yourself with that thing." He turned and walked away from the dumbstruck guard.

As Larry entered another gallery, he examined the key card he swiped from Brandon during their tussle. The kid's photograph was on one side and a magnetic strip was on the other. Then, after more searching, he spotted a way to use it. On the back wall was a door marked Employees Only. Larry glanced around to see if anyone was watching. Then he swiped the card through the security slot and pushed open the door.

Larry found himself in a maze of service corridors. As he made his way through, he kept looking for stairs leading down to the archives. So far he was out of luck and the clock was ticking.

As Larry turned a corner, he spotted two more security guards heading his way. Before they noticed him, he ducked into an employee locker room. As he waited for them to pass, his eyes fell over the rows of guard uniforms hanging on a rack. Larry smiled.

Two minutes later, he was back in the corridors. A sense of familiarity and comfort washed over him as he strode along with confidence. Larry was back in a security guard uniform. He grinned, enjoying the familiar weight of the flashlight as it bounced on his hip.

After making sure no one was in earshot, he pulled out his mobile phone and dialed Nick. "I'm in," he said when his son answered.

"Great," said Nick. "Where are you?"

"Northeast corridor of the Castle," Larry replied. "Just off the Commons. Now talk me through to the archives. Where am I going?"

Before Larry had left New York, he and Nick had come up with a plan to help navigate the Smithsonian. Once Larry found a way in, Nick would guide him using maps he was able to find on the Internet.

"Okay, there should be a stairwell coming up on the left," said Nick.

Larry jogged down the corridor until the stairwell came into view. "Got it." He ran down the stairs.

"Now it's kind of a maze down there," Nick warned. "Those underground tunnels connect a bunch of different buildings. It could get complicated."

"Yeah, well, we better move fast," said Larry. "Because sundown is in..." He checked his watch. "Twenty-eight minutes."

"Don't worry, Dad," his son reassured. "I'm going to talk you through it every step of the way. When you get down to B level, you're going to want to take a..." Nick's voice cut out.

Larry stopped. "Nicky? Nick?" He looked at his phone. There were no reception bars. Larry sighed and shoved it into his pocket. "I really should have factored in the whole below-ground thing." He hurried down the stairs.

At the bottom of the stairwell, Larry turned a corner and found his way barred by a chain-link fence. The dimly lit area contained a small speaker and security camera. While Larry checked the locked gate the speaker crackled.

"ID?" said a bored voice.

Larry quickly held up Brandon's key card. He made sure to hold it close to the camera, blocking himself from view.

"Brandon!" said the voice. "Going to Scruff's party tonight?"

Larry froze, trying to remember what the scruffy guard sounded like. Not quite sure, he winged it. "Yeah, totes," he replied. "Yo, can you buzz me in?"

"Aaa-ight," replied the voice.

A loud buzz sounded, followed by the click from the electronic lock. Larry pushed through the gate and into a large dark room beyond. The gate slammed shut behind him with an ominous *CLANG!* Its sound echoed all around him.

Larry didn't spot a light switch so he turned on his flashlight. The area was much bigger than he expected. There were columns of cabinets and rows of shelves as far as he could see. Crates too big for shelving were stacked in clearly marked rows forming narrow aisles. Wide corridors extended from either side of the large warehouse.

"Where are you, guys?" he asked.

Immediately, he spotted a large wooden crate. Since his friends had arrived the day before, maybe their container would be close to the entrance. Could he be that lucky? He threw off its canvas cover and opened a latch at the top. The front of the crate flew open.

Thwak! Thwa-thwak!

Several giant tentacles knocked him to the floor. Sitting on the ground, he found himself staring into the lifeless eye of a huge rubber squid. Larry sighed and scrambled over the spongy tentacles. He shoved them back into the crate, closing and latching the door. He wasn't so lucky after all.

Larry quickly moved through the dark corridors connecting more large storage areas. He zigzagged through an open space littered with tarp-covered antique cars and motorcycles. "Come on," he muttered impatiently. There was still no sign of his friends.

The next hall was a cleaning and restoration area. The Museum of Natural History in New York had a similar setup but this was ten times bigger. Paintings on easels were in various stages of being cleaned. Chipped vases and statues sat on different tables.

"You don't see that every day," he said, shining his light on the full-sized horse laid across a large countertop. It rested on its back with its legs stretched straight up. A tag dangling from one hoof read: Custer's Horse. The scene would have been comical if Larry hadn't turned and bumped into General Custer himself. The blond-haired mannequin wore a blue cavalry uniform and hat. He stood silently, smiling.

He moved past other displays, ready for cleaning. Another mannequin was a woman wearing a leather jacket with a wool collar. She had short brown hair and held an aviator hat and goggles. The placard on the nearby pedestal read: Amelia Earhart. First Female Pilot to Cross the Atlantic. Lost at Sea in 1937.

Jogging through another section, his flashlight beam flashed over a large Egyptian exhibit. Several full-sized mannequins held raised spears. A tall, thin man led the attack.

"Wait a minute," Larry said, sliding to a stop.

He shone the light on them once more. The warriors weren't posed at random, waiting to be cleaned or stored. They aimed their spears at a large metal cargo container—one large enough to house all his friends.

"Oh, man!" he said as he ran toward it.

He spotted a switch on the nearby wall and flipped it. Banks of fluorescent lights flickered and illuminated the frozen scene before him. Six Egyptian guards, dressed only in sandals and short white tunics, aimed sharp lances at the open end of the crate. Their leader, a pharaoh, wore a long gold tunic and an ornate royal headpiece. He stood front and center, pointing to the opening. His face was twisted with anger.

Larry threaded his way through the warriors and their sharp spears. He stepped over a phone, its cord stretching to the nearby wall. Its receiver was missing. Only its frayed cord remained.

Once at the container, he aimed his flashlight inside. Also frozen were his friends from the museum. Attila and his Hun warriors were in front, their swords held high. Jed stood atop a small crate, his tiny six-guns raised and ready. The Neanderthals and Sacajawea took cover in the back.

Dexter, meanwhile, stood atop a small crate inside the container. Clutched in his little furry hands was the Tablet of Ahkmenrah. The size of a large book, the tablet was made of solid gold. A small grid adorned its surface with a hieroglyphic image etched in each square.

"Troublemaker," Larry scolded the monkey. "We're going to talk about this later, Dexter."

Larry couldn't squeeze past the frozen Huns to reach the tablet. So he wrenched one of the spears away from an Egyptian and extended it into the container. Using the blunt end, he carefully pried the tablet from the monkey. It fell to the ground and he slid it toward him. Larry dropped the spear and grabbed the tablet. Then, as he backed away from the dark container, the Tablet of Ahkmenrah began to glow.

"No, no, no!" shouted Larry.

He was too late.

CHAPTER 3

"*Choruus!*" boomed a voice behind him. "*Tablet mah-rah!*"

Larry spun around and was face-to-face with the angry pharaoh. The ancient king signaled his men and they slammed the container shut. Then all spears were aimed at Larry's throat.

The pharaoh narrowed his eyes and leaned closer. He glared at Larry with suspicion, looking him up and down. At any moment he could order his men to skewer the former night guard like a pincushion. However, after a few more seconds, the pharaoh's face relaxed. "*Sprechen sie Deutsche?*" he asked in German. "*Parlez vous Francais?*" he asked in French. "English maybe?"

"Uh, yeah," replied Larry. "I speak English."

The pharaoh sighed. "Oh, thank goodness. My German is terrible." He held out a hand. "The tablet, if you please."

Larry pulled it to his chest. "I'm sorry, who are you?"

The man grinned as if waiting to be asked. "I am...Kahmunrah!" he boomed. "Great king of the great kings. And from the darkest depths of ancient history I have..." He thrust his arms high. "Come to life!"

"Uh-huh," said Larry.

Kahmunrah frowned. "Uh-huh?" he asked. "Did you not hear what I said? I am a centuries-old Egyptian pharaoh...come to life!"

"Yeah, I got that," Larry replied. He waved a hand dismissively. "Come to life, right."

The pharaoh shook his head in disbelief. "And you don't find that just the slightest bit...oh, I don't know." He leaned forward. *"SHOCKING?!!"*

"No need to yell," said Larry. "I'm standing right here. And the truth is, no. It's not so shocking. I mean, no offense, I know it's a big deal for you, coming to life and all. But it's less of a big deal for me."

The pharaoh eyed him suspiciously. "Just who are you?"

Larry extended a hand. "Larry Daley, Daley Devices." He lowered his hand when it was clear that Kahmunrah had no intention of shaking it. "Actually, I'm kind of tight with your brother Ahkmenrah back in the city. Good kid."

The pharaoh rolled his eyes. "Oh yes, my baby brother. The favorite son. Mother always gave him everything he wanted." He clenched his teeth. "Including the throne that was rightfully mine. Well..." He took a deep breath. "*Now* begins the era of Kahmunrah. So, give me the tablet!"

"Don't give it to him, Gigantor!" yelled Jed from the shipping container.

"Silence, miniature!" barked Kahmunrah. He put an arm around Larry's shoulders and led him away from the metal crate. "That tablet is more powerful than you, Larry Daley of Daley Devices, can possibly imagine. Bringing things to life is just a parlor trick. My brother was always too weak to embrace its full power." He stopped and spun to face him. "But with it, *I* shall unlock the gate to the Underworld. And bring my army from the Land of the Dead, where they have been waiting these three thousand years!" He held out his hand once more. "So, if you would be so kind as to hand it over."

"The tablet?" asked Larry.

"Yes, the tablet," replied the pharaoh. "Don't play dumb. Though you do it very well."

Larry had to think of a way to get away from the pharaoh and his men. Unfortunately, he didn't think he could outrun six flying spears. He had to come up with a plan. "Oh, all you want is the tablet?" he asked. "I thought you'd want...the cube."

"The cube?" asked Kahmunrah.

"Yeah, you know...the cube," Larry repeated. "The Cube of...Rubik. If all you want is the tablet then we're good. Here you go." He handed the tablet to Kahmunrah. "Knock yourself out. Have a good day in the Underworld." Larry waved and began to walk away.

"What is this Cube of Rubik?" asked Kahmunrah.

Larry turned back. "You know, the cube that turns all-who-oppose-you to dust? But that's cool. I know your brother didn't want to mess with it either. He liked to play it safe, too." He raised his hands. "No shame in that. I only mentioned it because you struck me as a *next-level* kind of guy."

Kahmunrah's eyes narrowed. "So where is this...cube, then?"

Larry laughed. "Seriously, man, you don't need to prove anything to me."

"I am not my brother," he growled. "I will kill you and your friends in the blink of an eye!"

Larry blinked. "A blink of an eye." He blinked again. "Because that is really fast. It's like..." He blinked again. "That fast?" He blinked three times quickly.

Kahmunrah trembled with anger. "Stop blinking and take me to the Cube of Rubik!"

Larry sighed. "All right."

With the Egyptians in tow, Larry retraced his steps. They followed him back to the first container he spotted. He whipped the tarp away and slapped the large wooden crate. "There you go."

The pharaoh laughed. "With the Tablet of Ahkmenrah and the Cube of Rubik, my power will know no bounds!"

Larry looked around. "Who are you talking to?"

Kahmunrah looked a little embarrassed. "Just generally. Everyone. It's kind of a reminder." He snarled. "I don't have to justify myself to you!" He pointed to the crate. "Now open it."

"You want *me* to open it?" asked Larry.

Kahmunrah smiled. "Just in case you were getting clever."

All spears were pointed at Larry once more. He didn't have a choice but to open it himself. He was hoping to avoid that. He stepped closer and thumbed the latch. He'd have to be very quick....

THWAP!

The door flew open. Larry barely made it clear as two giant tentacles sprung from the container. One thrashed about, sending the Egyptians flying. The other coiled around one of the guards, raising him high above the ground. It then flung him across the room. He slammed into a row of shelves.

THOOM!

The top of the crate exploded as the giant squid burst through. Eyes the size of dinner plates glared down as more tentacles lashed out at the Egyptians. Kahmunrah tried to run, but a tentacle struck like a snake. It slammed into his back, knocking the tablet from his grasp.

Larry darted forward. He leaped over one flailing appendage and ducked under another. He dove to the ground and slid across the floor. The tablet fell into his open arms. Larry scrambled to his feet and looked back at Kahmunrah. The pharaoh was busy prying himself out of a tentacle's grasp.

"I must have had the wrong crate," said Larry.

"I still have your friends!" Kahmunrah bellowed. He turned to his men. "Get me that tablet!" The tentacle tossed him out of sight.

Larry sprinted through the maze of storerooms and corridors. He tried to put some distance between himself and the pharaoh before doubling back to his friends. There was only one problem—Larry Daley was lost. Every crate-filled room looked the same.

Larry didn't know how lost he was until he turned a corner and saw the giant squid at the end of a long hallway. It slowly slithered toward him. Larry turned to retrace his steps when he saw the pack of Egyptian guards down the opposite corridor. He was trapped.

Suddenly, a loud roar filled the air. Larry looked up just as a motorcycle flew off a large shipping container. The bike had a sidecar and a very unusual driver—General George A. Custer. The famed Indian fighter held a staff flying his original cavalry flag. His long blond hair blew in the wind.

The motorcycle flew over Larry's head and skidded to a stop between him and the approaching Egyptians. Custer climbed into the sidecar. "Take the wheel!" he ordered.

As crazy as it seemed, Larry didn't really have a choice. The enemy was closing in. He leaped onto the bike.

Custer reached to the handlebars. "Just keep her straight and I'll handle the rest!" He hit the throttle and the bike lunged forward. "General George Custer, at the ready," he shouted. "Charge!!"

Larry barely stayed vertical as the bike barreled straight toward the Egyptians. "Wait, what's the plan here?" he asked.

The general grinned. "Who needs a plan? We're Americans! We don't plan! We do! When you build a house do you plan it first?"

"Actually, yes," replied Larry. "In detail. A *lot* of detail."

Custer laughed. "Nonsense! Details are for the weak!" He lowered his staff as if he were a knight on horseback. "Now hang on!"

Larry ducked as they slammed into the group of warriors. Tall men in tunics flew in every direction.

"See that? Act first, think later!" said Custer. "Works every time! You're in good hands. General George A. Custer of the Fighting U.S. 7th Cavalry!" He stood up in the sidecar. "Yeeeee-ha!"

WHAM!

The general slammed into a low shelf. He flew off the back of the motorcycle and tumbled to the ground. Larry glanced back to see him get to his feet, unfazed. "I'm all right!" he shouted. "Keep going, friend!"

Larry turned back and kept the bike on course. He clutched the tablet with one hand and controlled the throttle with the other. Then, as he rounded a corner, a figure stood directly in his path. It was all he could do to hit the brakes in time. The bike spun to one side, skidding to a screeching halt.

"What's the rumpus, Ace?" asked Amelia Earhart. The mannequin he had seen before never looked more vibrant and alive. She stood tall with her hands on her hips, radiating confidence and vigor.

"Listen, lady, I can't really stop right now," Larry explained.

"Lady? Who are you calling Lady?" she asked. "The name is Amelia."

THWUNK-TSSSSSSS!

The motorcycle rocked as a spear struck its back tire. The Egyptians had recovered and were closing in.

Amelia didn't seem to notice. "Amelia Earhart," she said. "You might have heard of me."

Larry climbed off the bike and ran down the corridor. Amelia kept pace. "Right, you were like this major pilot," he said.

"Pilot? I was the first woman to fly the Atlantic," she boasted. "First woman to receive the Flying Cross. First woman to fly across the forty-eight states." She didn't skip a beat as they turned a corner and sprinted between rows of shelves. "And now, if you'd wipe that perhaps permanent look of alarm off your kisser, I wonder if you might be so courteous as to tell me exactly where I am?"

"You're in a museum," replied Larry. "Actually under it. And *I'm* in a dangerous situation here. So, it might be best if you weren't anywhere near me."

Larry left her in the aisle as he ducked between two rows of shelves. He crouched behind a large crate to catch his breath. He glanced back; she was gone. Larry checked the other direction and jumped when he saw her crouching beside him. "Wow, you're fast," he said.

"What's your name, flyboy?" Amelia asked.

"Larry," he replied. "Larry Daley."

She stood and placed her hands on her hips. "Well, Larry Daley, in case you weren't listening, I'm not one to shy away from danger." Four spears impaled the wooden crate behind her. She didn't even flinch.

"How about spears?" he asked. "Are you one to shy away from spears?"

They took off down the aisle and dashed toward another corridor. When they turned the corner, three of the guards were dead ahead. Larry spotted a door to another stairwell midway between them and the warriors. A quick glance at Amelia told him she saw it, too.

She smiled. "Let's ankle, Skipper." She tossed her scarf around her neck and grabbed Larry's arm. She pulled him along as they sprinted toward the door. The Egyptians charged. They raised their spears, ready to intercept. Amelia chuckled. "Now we're going to have some fun!"

They ducked through the doorway and ran up the stairs. When they reached the top, they found themselves in the National Gallery of Art. They ducked through one of the connecting galleries, trying to increase their lead over the Egyptians.

"You're quite the popular fellow," said Amelia. "What do those scantily-clad gentlemen want with you anyway?"

Larry held up the tablet. "It's not me they want. It's this. And I can't let them have it."

"So why don't you just take it and skedaddle?" she asked.

"I can't just...skedaddle," he replied. "My friends are being held downstairs and I came here to help them." He scanned the gallery. "I need to find another way to get back down there."

SPLAT!

Something cold smacked Larry's face. Oddly enough, it felt like a snowball. Sure enough, he reached up and wiped clumps of packed snow from his sore cheek. He ducked as another whizzed by. He was surprised to see who threw it. "Okay, this is new."

It seemed as if the Tablet of Ahkmenrah affected paintings, as well. The one beside him was very much alive. A snowy scene in Central Park buzzed with winter activity. People threw snowballs, sledded down hills, and skated across a frozen pond. Larry leaned in for a closer look. A few of the little people pointed up at him and screamed. Larry waved. "Hey, I'm not going to hurt you guys."

"I don't think it's you they're afraid of, Mr. Daley," said Amelia.

Larry spun and saw three Egyptian guards enter the far side of the gallery. He and Amelia ducked and made a break for the opposite exit. They didn't get far before two more warriors cut them off. They were surrounded. All the guards moved in slowly. With spears raised, they herded Larry and Amelia into a corner.

Larry glanced back and saw they were near the famous painting, *American Gothic*. Alive as well, the famed older couple stood in front of their farmhouse and watched curiously. Larry reached into the painting and grabbed the man's pitchfork. "Can I borrow this for a second?" He pulled out the now full-sized trident. "Thanks!"

Larry aimed it at the guards. "Whoa, stop right there!" Unimpressed, they continued their slow advance. "I'll stick you like a bale of hay," Larry warned. "I'm serious. I'll do it!"

Amelia sighed. "Never send a boy to do a woman's job." She snatched the farming tool out of his hands. "I spent two weeks with a spear-hunting tribe in Micronesia. Watch and learn!" She reared back and flung it at the closest attacker. It sailed through the air with perfect precision. Unfortunately, the Egyptian caught it with ease. He spun it around and aimed it back at them. Amelia shrugged. "Of course, the Micronesians had much slower reflexes."

The men raised their own spears and began hurling them. Larry and Amelia ducked and moved along the wall. Lances stuck just above their heads. They dove for cover just as the pitchfork came flying back. They flew toward a wall of large photographs.

Larry raised his arm over his face, anticipating slamming into the wall. Instead, he felt himself falling much farther. He and Amelia never hit the wall but landed on hard cement instead.

Larry looked up to find they were in the middle of Times Square...and one heck of a party. All around people danced in the streets. Crowds cheered, streamers fell, and noisemakers rattled.

"Well this is one humdinger of a hootenanny," said Amelia.

Other than being transported back to New York, two things were very strange. One, everyone was dressed as they did in the forties, the men all in uniform. And two, everything, including Larry and Amelia, was in black and white. When Larry looked up and saw a sailor passionately kissing a nurse, he knew why. They were inside the famous photograph called "The Kiss." It was taken on V-J Day, at the end of World War II.

They looked back and saw a huge rectangular opening hovering in midair. Beyond the portal, he saw the museum, in color. And inside the museum, the Egyptians wrenched their spears from the wall and began to climb through. As they entered, they turned black and white, too.

Larry and Amelia pushed through the celebrating crowd. "Excuse me," he shouted. "Getting chased by crazy ancient Egyptians!" No one seemed to notice.

Larry felt his pocket vibrate and heard the ring of his cell phone. He pulled it out and was surprised to see an incoming call. "Oh, sure, I get four bars in 1945, but nothing in a stupid stairwell?!" As he snaked through the crowded street he calmly answered the phone. "Hello?"

He heard Nick's voice. "Dad! Finally! I've been redialing all night!"

"Hey, buddy," said Larry. He ducked just as a girl tried to hug him.

"So, listen," said Nick. "I've been studying these plans to the archives. It looks like once you get down the stairwell..."

Larry glanced back. The Egyptians pushed through the crowd after them. "Oh, I'm way past the stairwell, Nicky."

"You found everyone?" asked Nick.

"Sort of," replied Larry. He and Amelia pushed further into the mob.

"What is that fibbledy-widget you're talking to?" asked Amelia.

"Who is that, Dad?" asked Nick.

"It's nobody," replied Larry.

Amelia stopped and placed her hands on her hips. "What do you mean, *nobody?*" she asked. "I am very much a somebody!"

Larry reached back and grabbed her arm. "It's Amelia Earhart," he told Nick as he pulled her along.

"You found Amelia Earhart?" Nick asked.

Suddenly, Amelia was pulled from his grasp. A sailor took her in his arms and danced away with her. "Nicky, I have to call you later," said Larry.

Before he could go after her, Larry slammed into a husky sailor. The phone flew from his hand. "What's your hurry, bub?" asked the sailor. "Didn't you hear? The war's over!"

"Not for me," said Larry. He pointed at the Egyptians. "Those guys are trying to catch me."

"Really?" The sailor glanced at the Egyptians then back at Larry. "What unit you from?"

"Uh, I'm from Brooklyn," said Larry. The guards were closing fast.

"Yeah?" The sailor grinned. "I'm from Flatbush!" He turned and gave a loud whistle. "Hey, fellas!" Sailors all around them turned to look. The first one pointed to the Egyptians. "These guys are trying to beat up my buddy here, just because he's from Brooklyn!"

The sailors yelled as they swarmed over the guards. An odd brawl developed, pitting World War II soldiers against centuries-old Egyptian warriors. Oddly enough, Larry had seen stranger things. He made his way back toward the portal while the guards were distracted. He didn't see Amelia anywhere.

Unfortunately, it didn't take long for a few of the Egyptians to muscle away from the throng of sailors. They doubled back, scanning the crowd. They had yet to spot him but were closing fast. If he didn't do something, they'd catch him for sure.

Larry made it back to the sailor kissing the nurse. He tapped the man on the shoulder. "Sorry, I just need to do this." He pushed the man aside and kissed the nurse in the same way. The Egyptians ran by as he held the embrace.

"Anytime you're done in there, Mr. Daley!" Amelia shouted from outside the photo. She reached in and grabbed Larry's jacket, pulling him toward the opening.

Larry caught his breath. "Thank you," he told the nurse. "That was very... helpful."

"Call me!" she yelled after him.

Larry was yanked out of the photograph. Back in the museum and in full color, he fell to the floor at Amelia's feet. The pilot crossed her arms and smirked. "Well, I wouldn't have thought it to look at you, but you're quite the smooth operator."

Larry shrugged and got to his feet. "I had to think of something."

Amelia pointed to the photo. "Well, keep thinking because here they come!" The Egyptian warriors charged toward them in the photo. Soon they would be free, too.

"I have an idea." Larry pointed to the photo's frame. "Get that side!" Together, they each grabbed a side of the large photograph. They pulled it away from the wall, swinging it out on its long cable. "One... two... three!" In unison, they flipped the frame around and slammed it back against the wall. A loud thud rocked the gallery as the guards slammed into the wall. They were trapped inside the photo.

"Wow, that actually worked," said Larry. "Thank you."

Amelia grinned. "What's next?"

"What's next is...I head back downstairs, grab my friends, and try to get out of here." Larry moved toward the gallery exit.

"Well then..." Amelia followed him. "Let's hightail it, Cappie!"

Larry stopped and held out a hand. "Look, nothing personal, but I'm kind of in the middle of something here that's not really your fight."

Amelia glared at him. "It's because I'm a woman, isn't it?"

"No." Larry shook his head. "It's because I've got this ancient raised-from-the-dead-evil-pharaoh guy who's willing to kill me and probably anyone near me to get this tablet so he can rule the world!"

She raised an eyebrow. "So it is because I'm a woman."

"Look—" Larry began.

"No, *you* look, Mr. Daley!" She poked his chest with her finger. "If it weren't for me, you'd still be lost in that monochromatic mayhem."

"Lost in what?" asked Larry.

"The black-and-white photograph, you boob," she replied. "Now listen and listen good. I want to help you. Not because I like you, which so far I don't. But because I smell adventure, Mr. Daley, and I want in!"

Larry sighed. "Okay, fine." He continued toward the exit. "But don't blame me if something happens to you."

Amelia laughed as she followed. "I should be so lucky!"

CHAPTER 4

Kahmunrah was furious that his men never returned. However, instead of having a temper tantrum (something he did often, back in the palace) he came up with a plan.

"I am Kahmunrah, half-god-once-removed on my mother's side," the pharaoh explained. "Ruler of Egypt. Future ruler of...well...everything else. I've lost my men, so I need some new generals to join me in my plan to conquer this world." He nodded approvingly. "I have studied your placards and I have selected *you*."

Standing before him were three notorious men from history. Ivan the Terrible, the fearsome Russian czar, was tall, wore a long gold robe, and held an ornate staff. He had long black hair and a stringy beard to match.

Napoléon Bonaparte kept one hand tucked in his shirt while the other smoothed down his short black hair. He was a devious military commander and self-imposed emperor of France. He was short and wore a white and blue uniform with a chestful of medals.

Al Capone, the 1920s American gang leader, licked his thick lips, ready for action. He wore a dark pin-stripe suit and matching fedora. Whereas Ivan and Napoléon were mannequins come to life, Capone was different. The young gangster had been a life-sized photograph. He was completely in black and white.

"Ivan the Terrible, Napoléon Bonaparte, and Al Capone," said Kahmunrah. "Some of the most evil and feared leaders in history." He smiled widely. "Gentlemen, really, really fantastic to meet you!"

"And me you," replied Ivan.

Capone nodded. "I've heard good things."

"Wonderful to meet you finally," Napoléon said with a crisp bow.

"All I ask is your allegiance," continued the pharaoh. "In return, I offer you the world!" He clasped his hands together and leaned forward. "Any questions?"

"Yeah, I got one," said Capone. He pointed to the pharaoh's outfit. "How come you're wearing a dress?"

Kahmunrah shook his head. "It's not a dress. It's a tunic," he explained. "It was the height of fashion three thousand years ago. Any other questions?"

"Yes," said Ivan. "This, uh...dress you are wearing. Do we have to wear one, too?"

Kahmunrah grimaced. "No, you don't have to wear one, too." He tried to keep his temper in check. "And as I just told Mr. Capone, it's not a dress. It's a tunic. Big difference."

He turned to the others. "Any other questions?" Napoléon's hand shot up. The pharaoh sighed. "Any questions *not* about the dress?" He caught himself. "Tunic!" Napoléon lowered his hand.

Al Capone smiled and cracked his knuckles. "Uh, yeah, is there going to be killing? Because I'm really good at the killing." He smiled at the others. "It's kind of my niche."

Ivan raised a finger before the pharaoh could answer. "I first want to clarify something," said the former czar. "People always say, 'Ivan the

71

Terrible, he's so terrible. I'm so scared of Ivan. He's bad news.' When in fact, the correct translation is *Ivan the Awesome*."

"Yes," said Kahmunrah. "But it's not as catchy."

Ivan stroked his long beard. "But I wasn't terrible. I was quite an effective leader, actually. I created the first Russian army. I introduced the printing press, transformed Russia into a multiethnic state—"

"Didn't you murder your son?" asked Napoléon.

Ivan nodded calmly. "You say tomato..." Then he loomed over Napoléon in anger. "And I say...*I will tear off your head if you ever mention that again!*"

Kahmunrah clapped. "So, gentlemen, are you with me?"

"Yeah, sure," replied Capone.

"*Da*," agreed Ivan in Russian.

Napoléon nodded. "*Oui*."

"Superb," said the pharaoh. "Then bring Larry Daley of Daley Devices and the golden tablet to me!"

Jedediah looked up at the new prisoner in their midst. Of all people, it was General Custer. Apparently, he had tried to help Larry before being captured by Kahmunrah's men. The general from the Wild West was famous for his defeat at Little Big Horn. Jed didn't know how he planned to help them escape.

"All right, troops," said Custer. He addressed the huddled New York exhibits. "When your enemies captured me, they made themselves *my* enemies, as well. Here's what we're going to do!" He held up a bugle. "On the third bugle blast, I shall loudly announce..." He glanced around then whispered, "Attack." A wide grin spread across his face. "Then we shall dive out of this box and attack! What do you think?"

Jed looked at Octavius and rolled his eyes.

"I know I'm just a tracker and you're a general," said Sacajawea. "But won't yelling *attack* alert them that we're about to attack?"

Jed pulled Octavius aside. "Okay, Kemo Sabe, listen up." He pointed up at Custer. "This rodeo clown wouldn't know a flapjack from a flyswatter. Gigantor is out there risking his hide to save us. The least we can do is try and get help. Big help. And we can't very well do that locked up in here, now can we?"

Octavius put on his helmet and beat a fist against his metal chest plate in a Roman salute. He pointed to a small rusted-out hole at the bottom of the shipping container. "Yes," he agreed with a smile. "We must make our escape."

Larry had to find a way to circle back and help his friends. Kahmunrah's men were now trapped in the photograph. Getting past one snobbish pharaoh shouldn't be a problem. He and Amelia ran through the art museum. They passed more living works of art. Marble and bronze statues strolled freely while paintings everywhere were buzzing with activity.

They ran into a large hall with a giant fountain in the center. However, just as they reached the fountain, several soldiers entered from the opposite side. They wore blue and white uniforms and held long muskets armed with sharp bayonets. The Napoléonic soldiers looked out of place as they pushed through several living statues. The men scanned the gallery looking for something...or someone. Larry hated to believe it, but it was clear the soldiers were working for the pharaoh.

Larry grabbed Amelia's shoulders and pulled her down beside the fountain. "Since when did the French fight with the Egyptians?" he asked.

Amelia shrugged. "World War I, World War II, the Algerian War for Liberation..."

"Okay, I was being rhetorical," said Larry.

Amelia chuckled. "You were being misinformed."

Larry shushed her. "Why don't you keep it down?"

She smiled. "Well, well, Mr. Daley. I quite like the way you're holding me."

"What? No, I'm not," said Larry. Then he realized that he still held her shoulders. He let go. "I was just...Sorry, I didn't mean to."

"Stop beating your gums, Mr. Daley," she said, giving him a playful shove. "You haven't been able to take your cheaters off me since the moment we met."

Larry stared at her. "I didn't understand one word of that."

Amelia grinned. "If you say so." Then she glanced around. "Is it just me, or is there music in the air?"

Larry heard it, too. "No, it's not just you." He heard a soft harp and what sounded like children humming. He glanced up and saw where it came from. "There is *literally* music in the air."

Three marble cherubs hovered above them. One of the winged babies plucked the strings of a small lyre. The other two hummed along to the gentle melody.

"Hey, guys. Baby angels," Larry whispered. "Whatever you are."

"They're Cupids, Mr. Daley," Amelia corrected. "The gods of love." She gazed into his eyes.

Larry sighed. "Okay, gods of love. Could you stop that? We're trying to hide here."

The cherubs glanced at one another and stopped playing. Then the one with the lyre shrugged and began a different tune. The others joined in.

"The secret to happiness is . . ."

"Where are we?"

"Tick-tock, Mr. Daley. Your hour's begun."

"Since when did the French fight with the Egyptians?"

"I'm thinking, I'm thinking, I'm thinking . . ."

Able snatched the tablet when Larry wasn't looking.

"Time to paint the town red!"

"Mr. Daley, are you coming or what?"

"And now, after three thousand years, my evil empire shall be ... unleashed!"

"We are *not* going to attack right now!"

"*This* is your Last Stand."

Home at last.

"No, no. It's not the arrangement," said Larry. He peeked over the fountain's edge. The soldiers pointed at the floating cherubs. They began making their way toward the fountain. "Great," Larry told them. "Thanks for alerting them to our presence through song."

One of the cherubs shoved another one. "You were flat," he accused.

"I wasn't flat," said the second cherub. "You were sharp. Trust me, it was painful to listen to."

"Guy, guys!" shouted the third Cupid. He whipped out his bow and arrow and began shooting arrows at the other two.

"Ow! Ow!" They shouted, even though the tiny arrows bounced off their marble behinds.

Larry grabbed Amelia's hand. "Come on. We have to move." Still crouching, they moved along the large fountain as the soldiers rounded the other side.

While the soldiers investigated the cherubs, Larry and Amelia dashed toward the nearest exit. They turned a corner and screeched to a halt in front of Napoléon himself. The short man clicked his heels together and gave a curt bow.

"You are now my prisoners," he announced. The former emperor reached for his sword. "*En garde!*" Instead of unsheathing his sword, he only whipped out the small hilt with no blade attached. "Oh, great," he said with disgust. He dropped the hilt and produced a small dagger. He aimed it at Larry. "Now, you will come with me, little man."

Larry laughed. "Little man? Really? *You're* calling *me* little?"

"Yes I am, little man." He puffed out his chest. "You are now the captive of the great Napoléon Bonaparte."

Larry held up his hands. "Hey, I'm just saying...you're actually famously little." Larry chuckled. "There's literally a complex named after how little you are."

Napoléon lowered his dagger. "Oh, please! I'm almost as tall as you."

"No you're not," Larry argued. He gestured to the man's hat. "Maybe with the hat. That's half a foot right there."

Napoléon whipped off his hat. "You just have puffier hair." He stood on his tiptoes, then pointed a finger. "I command you to turn around!"

Larry turned while Napoléon backed up to him. They stood back-to-back. "Fetching lady," said Napoléon. "Who is taller?"

"Hmm...it's very close," said Amelia.

While Napoléon's back was turned, Larry seized the opportunity. He grabbed Amelia's hand and ran toward another gallery. When they turned the corner, once again, they slid to a stop. Four of Napoléon's soldiers waited for them. They leveled their sharp bayonets at the couple.

Napoléon strolled in behind them. "And so, the little tiny man, who couldn't be a *shorter* mouse, runs into the claws of the *giant* cat."

"Okay," said Larry. "You have height issues. I get it."

Bonaparte sneered. "You are a naive American manboy. I, one of the great tactical minds of all time, challenged you to a back-to-back-who's-taller. I *knew* you would try to flee." He grinned. "Right into my snare!"

"Snazzy maneuver, Emperor," said Amelia.

He nodded. "Thank you, Mademoiselle." He looked back at Larry. "And now if your boyfriend would kindly come with me."

"Look, I'm not her boyfriend," said Larry. "We just met."

Napoléon rolled his eyes. "Whatever." He extended a hand. "Now, this way or you die."

With the bayonets aimed at his back, Larry began to follow Napoléon. Then Amelia jumped in front of them. "I'm coming with you," she said.

The former emperor stopped and bowed. "Mademoiselle, our fight is not with you." He clicked his heels together again. "I bid you *adieu*."

Napoléon and his men led Larry out of the gallery. He nudged Larry with an elbow. "She definitely likes you," he said with a snicker. Larry looked back to see Amelia gazing at him.

CHAPTER 5

L arry was taken back to the Castle and the Mythic Door to the Underworld display. He saw that Napoléon and his soldiers weren't the only mannequins Kahmunrah had recruited. Ivan the Terrible was there along with a few of his Streltsi soldiers. Larry also noticed a young Al Capone and several of the gang leader's henchmen. As Larry and his captors approached, he saw he wasn't the only prisoner.

"Hey, boss," said one of Capone's henchmen. "We found this one trying to escape through a rust hole in the crate." He held up a small birdcage. Inside, sitting on the swing, was Jedediah. "One of his little friends got away, though."

Kahmunrah waved him off. "Please. What damage could they do? They're no bigger than a grain of couscous."

Larry guessed the *little friend* must have been Octavius.

Kahmunrah took the cage from the henchman. "You're in luck, tiny cowboy. Just in time to see me take my rightful place as ruler of everything."

"Can't wait," Jedediah said sarcastically.

The pharaoh set the cage down as Larry was brought forward. He reached out and snatched the tablet from Larry's hands. "I'll take this, thank you."

He moved to the Door to the Underworld, spun around, and raised the tablet triumphantly. "Behold! The Tablet of Ahkmenrah! Our key to unleashing the Horus!" He pointed to etchings on the door. They depicted wicked warriors with bodies of men and heads of hawks.

Larry tried to look unimpressed. "Gee, you sure are loud," he said.

The pharaoh smiled. "They are my powerful army of the underworld. With them we shall take over the world!" He turned and placed the tablet into the impression. It fit perfectly. "And now, after three thousand years, my evil army shall be...unleashed!" Kahmunrah pressed the series of symbols on the tablet and jumped back.

Nothing happened.

The pharaoh rushed forward and pressed the combination again. "I said...my evil army shall be..." He leaped back once more. "Unleashed!"

Again, nothing happened.

Kahmunrah laughed nervously. "It's an old key. Sometimes you have to jiggle it a little." He reached up and jiggled the tablet. Then he pressed the symbols in a different series. "Come on, talk to papa. Mother and father must have changed the combination."

"Guess they didn't trust you," Larry commented.

Napoléon looked puzzled. "So, no taking over the world?"

"Give me a moment!" barked Kahmunrah.

"Is it the killing time yet?" asked Al Capone.

"No, it's not the killing time!" the pharaoh replied. "When it's the killing time, I will say *Mr. Capone, it's the killing time*." He tapped the tablet some more. "Right now I just need to figure out the new combination."

"Excuse me?" said Ivan the Terrible. He pointed to the tablet. "What's all that scribbling on it? Perhaps they left some kind of clue."

"I don't know what it is," Kahmunrah replied. "I don't read Egyptian."

"What do you mean?" asked Ivan. "You don't read?" He turned to Larry and shrugged. "Reading is the key to imagination."

"Reading is boring!" the pharaoh growled. "Besides, I had a royal reader." His fingers flew over the symbols. "Let's see. Father's birthday, 6.19.1105 B.C."

Larry shook his head and laughed. Here he was worried that this guy could really take over the world. Larry sat down on a nearby bench, relieved.

Kahmunrah reeled on him. "What are you laughing at?"

"Nothing." Larry shook his head. "I'm just taking a load off. I'm sorry this whole unleashing-the-underworld thing didn't work out for you." He checked his watch. "Anyway, in a couple of hours, you'll be frozen in some angry position. Then I'll take my buddies out of here and that'll be that." He grinned. "I have all night."

Kahmunrah turned toward Jedediah's cage. "Well, *he* doesn't." The pharaoh opened the

cage and snatched up the miniature cowboy.
He marched over to another display and grabbed
a large brass hourglass. He popped off the top
and dropped Jedediah inside. He replaced the
lid and flipped the hourglass over. Sand began
to pour onto the tiny cowboy. "From the looks
of this, I'd say he has a little over an hour."

Larry got to his feet. "What are you doing?"

Kahmunrah plucked the tablet from the door
and handed it to Larry. "You were the guard.
You know this tablet," he said. "You may not
know the combination, but I'm giving you an
hour to figure it out. If you don't, I kill *all* your
friends. And don't even think about escaping.
I'll be watching."

"Wait, no," Larry protested. "I don't know
how to figure this out."

"Pity," said the pharaoh. He shook the
hourglass, knocking Jed to his knees. "Your little
cowboy friend seemed a charming fellow.
Ticktock, Mr. Daley. Your hour's begun."

"You got this, partner," yelled Jed through
the glass. "I know you do."

Larry went back downstairs to the archives. Through the series of tunnels, he made his way to the Smithsonian's Natural History Museum. Maybe there was some Egyptian exhibit that could help him decipher the tablet. He was running out of time and ideas.

As he emerged from the stairwell, he almost ran smack into Amelia Earhart. "Are you all right?" she asked. "I was worried sick. Sick, I tell you."

Larry kept moving. "Yeah, I'm fine."

"Boffo, Billy!" said Amelia. "Glad to hear it!" She fell into step as he moved about the museum. "You know, I went on a little expedition and found the crate containing your friends. It's being guarded by a couple of two-cent toughies. But we can take them! I know we can!"

"We can't do that," said Larry. "I have to get this tablet translated right now."

"Chin up, Captain," she said. "I found myself in fog thicker than pea soup over the Atlantic, and somehow made it through that mess. We'll lick this yet."

"Well, unless you speak Egyptian we're not licking anything," said Larry.

"Hello?" called a familiar voice. "Some assistance here?"

Larry turned the corner to see a life-sized bust of Teddy Roosevelt. The animated marble head sat on a tall pedestal. It was wonderful to see a familiar face. Teddy had helped him during his first night as a night guard. He couldn't have come across a better person...or the head of a better person.

"Teddy! Perfect," said Larry. He ran up to the bust. "I could really use your help right now."

"And I'd be happy to help you, sir," said Teddy. "But first things first. My nose is so itchy, it's making me insane! I hate to ask. But as you can see, I'm minus a few body parts. So, could you...please?"

"Oh, uh...sure," said Larry. He tentatively reached up and scratched Teddy's nose.

"Sweet rutabaga pie, that's divine!" yelled Teddy. "Yes!" He grinned. "Thank you, young man. That was exquisite. Theodore Roosevelt—"

"Twenty-sixth president, Rough Rider, founder of the national parks, and a bunch of other stuff," Larry finished for him.

The bust eyed him suspiciously "I'm sorry, have we met?"

"Oh no," said Larry. "There's another Teddy... well, we have one of you in New York, too."

"I see," said the bust. "And, what's he like? This other me."

"Uhh...a lot like you, I guess," replied Larry. "Except with...you know..."

"Say it," said the Teddy bust. He shook his head. "He has a body, doesn't he?"

Larry cringed. "And a horse."

Teddy rolled his eyes. "Dash it, that hurts! That's just salt in the wound!"

"Sorry," said Larry. "Look, I really need you to translate what's written on this tablet." He held it up. "Do you read hieroglyphics?"

"Of course," said the Teddy bust. He scanned the symbols. "Oh yes. This is a simple one. Bird...man with spear...sideways fish...beetle... vase."

"So, what does it mean?" asked Amelia.

Teddy raised an eyebrow. "It means...and this is a rough translation...a man with a spear is trying to trap a bird and a sideways fish in a vase. And also there's a beetle."

Larry sighed. "Yeah, I don't think that that's what it actually means."

"That's *one* possible translation," Teddy added. "Another possible translation: You will find the combination you seek, if you figure out the secret at the heart of the pharaoh's tomb."

"Okay, so what does *that* mean?" asked Larry.

"I don't know!" barked Teddy. "What's this? What's that? Why don't you ask New York Teddy?" He frowned. "I'm sure he'd like to get his grubby little hands and feet all over that thing. Probably let his horse lick it, too."

Amelia pulled Larry away from the bust. "Mr. Daley, I think we should head to the sculpture hall."

"Why?" asked Larry.

"There's someone there who might have a better thought on this," she replied.

"Hang on a second," said Larry. He turned back to the bust. "Hey, Teddy, one last thing. Before I came here, the Teddy Roosevelt in New York was about to tell me something. It seemed pretty important. He said that the secret to happiness is...blank. Any idea what he was going to say?"

"The secret to happiness?" asked the bust. His mouth tightened. "Oh, I'll tell you the secret to happiness. It's having a body!" he yelled.

Larry cringed and backed away. The Teddy bust kept up the tirade. "Being more than just a head!" Teddy shouted. "What do you think about that? *That's* the secret to happiness!"

Larry heard the bust's rant as he and Amelia ran through the museum. Before long, they found themselves in the sculpture hall. Even though Larry had seen the exhibits come to life every night at his old job, he was amazed to see the many sculptures walking around.

Amelia pulled Larry through the crowd of living statues. "The fellow we're looking for is just down here," she said. Then she ground to a halt as a bronze ballerina danced in front of her. "Well, hello, young lady," said Amelia.

Larry pushed past the statue. "Can we please keep moving?" he asked. "I've got a little person stuck in an hourglass, an ancient combination lock to crack, and a huge business meeting in a matter of hours. We have to move here."

Amelia pointed past him. "There he is!"

Larry looked up and saw the famous sculpture by Auguste Rodin. The large bronze man sat on a stone with his chin resting on one fist. It was *The Thinker*.

Larry and Amelia rushed up to the huge man. Amelia tapped him on the side. "Mr. Thinker, we don't mean to interrupt your contemplation," she said. "But we have something of a conundrum to crack and I wonder if we might run it by you."

The Thinker looked down at them. "How you doing?" he asked in a deep, not so intelligent-sounding voice.

"Just dandy, sir," replied Amelia. "But right now we need to figure out the secret that's at the heart of the pharaoh's tomb."

"I'm, The Thinker," said the statue. "By Ro...Ro-dian." He had trouble pronouncing the artist's name.

"Yes, sir, we know," said Amelia. "That's why we're asking." She pointed to the tablet. "Any thoughts on what this secret might be?"

"The secret?" asked The Thinker.

"The one I just asked you about," she reminded. "The one at the heart of the pharaoh's tomb."

He put his head back down on his chin. "I'm thinking, I'm thinking, I'm thinking...."

Larry noticed The Thinker looking past them to a beautiful Venus statue. "What's happening here?" asked Larry.

"He's thinking," said Amelia.

"Wow," said The Thinker. "Check *her* out."

Larry snapped his fingers in front of the statue's face. "Oh, come on!" he said. "This is serious."

"Apparently, it's a matter of life and death," Amelia added.

"I'll tell you what's a matter of life and death," said the statue. He slowly stood. "That beautiful lady over there." He waved. "Hello, gorgeous!" Venus smiled back at him.

Larry threw up his arms. "This guy is totally distracted."

The Thinker flexed his muscles. "Hey, baby! Check out the gun show over here!" He raised an arm and kissed a bicep.

Amelia sighed. "He's certainly no Einstein."

Larry spun around. "Yes, but *Einstein* is Einstein!" He paced back and forth. "I saw a bunch of Einsteins..." He couldn't remember where they'd been. There were tons of them. He could still see their little heads bobbing up and down.

Then it hit him. He grabbed Amelia's hand and ran to the window. He pointed across the National Mall to the Air and Space Museum. "There," he said. "Air and Space. In the gift shop!"

Amelia smiled. "And so the adventure continues!"

"Yes, great. The adventure continues," Larry agreed. Then he noticed Amelia still gazing at him. "Why are you staring at me?"

"I don't want to miss a moment," she replied.

Larry held up his hands. "Okay, look. I think you're great and a really, really attractive person. But there's a laundry list of reasons why you shouldn't be looking at me like that."

Just then, soft music filled the air. It was full of gentle plucking strings and the humming of tiny voices. Larry sighed and looked up. Sure enough, the cherubs hovered above. The small cupids couldn't resist taking advantage of another romantic moment.

"Hello again," said Larry. "Okay, yes, very pretty. But not really appropriate." The cherubs

frowned and began to play a different song.
Larry shook his head. "Okay, can you just fly
away now? Please?"

Embarrassed, Larry turned back to Amelia.
"Look, about that..." She was smiling at him
again. "What?"

"You don't let yourself enjoy things much,"
she said. "Do you, Mr. Daley?"

"That's not...," he began to protest.
"Look...," he started, but became flustered.
"Okay, forget it. Can we just focus here?"

Amelia laughed. "Okay," She marched
toward the door. "Let's go meet Mr. Einstein!"

Octavius trudged through the dense lawn.
The tiny soldier had been traveling for hours but
still hadn't seen an end to the thick carpet of
grass. "I promised Jedediah to bring help," he
said. "And help I shall bring." He didn't know
whom he would find, but he couldn't let his
friends down.

However, for the past few feet, he felt as if he
wasn't alone. In fact, he felt as if someone or

some *thing* was stalking him. He peered into the darkness but could see no one.

Crack.

A twig snapped behind him. The commander froze. He listened for a moment but heard nothing but the wind. Sensing danger, he drew his sword and whirled around. "Who's there?" he asked.

He saw only darkness.

Then a large shadow spread across him. Gripping his sword tightly, Octavius slowly turned to see a giant beast looming above. "Jupiter protect me," he whispered.

The creature was covered with reddish brown fur and stared down at him with giant black eyes. Two long, sharp teeth jutted from its mouth, and fierce claws extended from its paws. The squirrel leaned forward to get a closer look at the tiny Roman. Its hot breath blew across the man's face as it sniffed him.

"Remain very still," Octavius whispered to himself. "It can sense movement."

The squirrel reared back and chirped loudly. To Octavius's tiny ears, it sounded like the fierce roar of a lion. The beast flicked its bushy tail and crouched, ready to strike.

"And apparently it can hear me talking to myself," he added. He held his sword ready, preparing for battle.

With lightning-fast speed, the squirrel reached out and swiped the sword from the commander's hand. Octavius grabbed for his lost weapon, but the beast easily swatted him away. The tiny man tumbled backward.

Before Octavius could get to his feet, the squirrel grabbed him by the ankle. It scampered away, dragging him across the lawn.

"Nooooooooooo!" shouted Octavius as it pulled him into the dark bushes.

CHAPTER 6

"Oh no!" cried Kahmunrah. "Earthquake! Earthquake!"

He laughed as he shook the hourglass. The tiny cowboy struggled to stay on his feet. All the while, the sand continued to pour onto his puny head. Already the level was almost to his waist. It wouldn't be long before he was buried completely.

Kahmunrah brought the specimen closer. "You must feel so powerless being the plaything of my whim," Kahmunrah said. Then he bellowed with laughter.

"You just keep flapping your yap-trap, Koo Koo Roo," Jedediah said defiantly. "You and me are going to tussle *real* soon."

The pharaoh laughed harder at such a pitiful threat.

"You should probably come look at this," said Napoléon. He stood near the window. "I think we have problems."

Kahmunrah gave the hourglass another shake before setting it down. Then he joined Napoléon at the window. He saw Larry Daley and some woman across the Mall. They were leaving the Natural History Museum.

The pharaoh's face twisted with anger. "He's trying to escape with the tablet!" He spun around and aimed a finger at the Russian czar. "Ivan. Send your men to stop them!"

The pharaoh was filled with rage. Some lowly night guard wouldn't thwart his grand plans. He marched over and gave the hourglass another shake for good measure. When Ivan's men brought Larry back, he'd make the night guard watch all his friends suffer.

Every single one of them.

Larry and Amelia ran onto the manicured lawn of the National Mall. The night air was crisp, and moonlight lit the way as they headed toward the Air and Space Museum.

Suddenly, Amelia grabbed Larry's arm. "Crimeny!" she shouted as she brought him to a halt. "We're jimmy-jacked!"

She pointed toward the Castle. A group of men poured out of the side entrance. They carried lanterns and were making a beeline for Larry and Amelia.

Larry didn't run. Instead, he turned to Amelia. "Jimmy-jacked?" he asked. "Really?"

Amelia shrugged. "It's the way I speak."

"Yeah, but *jimmy-jacked*?" He shook his head. "I don't know. That one definitely sounds made up. Even for you."

Amelia rolled her eyes. "Oh no. Our path has been blocked by bad people," she said very formally. "What's the fun in talking like that?" She pointed back toward the men. "The point is we're not getting into Air and Space right now."

Larry saw the lanterns moving closer. They illuminated the men carrying them. There were four men in heavy coats and pointed hats carrying long swords. They looked like Ivan the Terrible's men.

"Yeah, we're pretty jimmy-jacked," said Larry. "Follow me." He took off toward the Washington Monument.

He led the way, past the monument and into the Lincoln Memorial. They climbed the steps of the open pavilion and hid behind one of the tall columns. The huge marble structure was quiet and peaceful.

"We should be okay hiding in here for a while," said Larry. He sat with his back to one of the columns.

Amelia joined him. "So, how long have you guarded antiquities?"

"What?" asked Larry. "Oh no. I don't actually work here."

She pointed to his jacket. "I just thought with the fancy getup and all."

Larry glanced down at his uniform. "Yeah, no, I just borrowed this. I mean... I *was* a guard, back in New York. But that was a while ago."

"Why did you leave?" she asked. "Did you not enjoy it?"

"No, I loved it," he replied. "But things sort of took off in another direction."

"And what are you now?" she asked.

"I have my own business," he said proudly. "I sort of design products and sell them."

Her eyes lit. "So you're an inventor?"

"Sure, yeah. I guess," he replied. "I invent things."

"Like the rocket ship?" she asked.

Larry shook his head. "No, not so much that."

"A seaplane, maybe?" she guessed. "A dirigible?"

"No, not aircraft," said Larry.

"Oh, something scientific." She clasped her hands together. "How noble! Have you discovered a cure for polio?"

Larry shook his head. "No, but someone else did." He glanced around. "I'm more small scale. Have you ever heard of the Glow-in-the-Dark Flashlight?" he asked. He held a thumb to his chest. "Well, I invented it. Some other stuff, too."

Amelia stared at him blankly. Then she leaned closer. "And this new job of yours...you like it?"

"Yeah, it's going real well, actually," he replied. He tried to sound excited. "It'll be going even better if I actually get to this big meeting, which is in"—he checked his watch—"four hours. But yeah, it's pretty exciting."

Amelia stared at him with a puzzled expression.

"What?" he asked.

"I'm confused," she replied. "If you're not excited by it, then why do you do it?"

"I just said I was excited," Larry explained.

"I know what you *said*, Mr. Daley." She cocked her head. "But what I see in front of me is someone who has lost his moxie."

"No, no, I have my moxie," Larry said. "I have a *lot* of moxie." What Larry *didn't* have was a chance to see the tablet glowing in his arms.

Amelia chuckled and turned away. Suddenly, her eyes widened and her mouth gaped open. "Great Gatsby," she said, looking up. She scrambled to her feet.

"Where the devil did I put my hat?" asked a booming voice.

Larry spun around to see the giant marble statue of Abraham Lincoln come to life. The huge man leaned over the side of his chair, searching for his hat. Larry had forgotten he held the Tablet of Ahkmenrah. Bringing it so close made the statue come to life, as well. The enormous former president stood and leaned forward, peering out from between the columns.

Larry leaped to his feet. "Oh no. Please, Mr. President! Don't get up on our account!" He held his hands up in front of the statue. "I can't let you go out there! If anyone sees you like this, it'll really freak a lot of people out."

"Freak them out?" asked Lincoln. "I assure you, I am no freak, sir." The giant statue reached down and grabbed Larry by the back of the collar. He held Larry up for a closer look. "In fact, if anyone is freakish, it's you. The truth is, you are small, even for a regular-sized human."

"What?" asked Larry. "Why would you say that?"

Lincoln shrugged. "I must be honest."

"Right." Larry threw up his hands. "Honest Abe. Great."

Amelia stepped forward. "Come now, Mr. President. Put the little man down and let's sit our fanny back in that throne of yours!"

Lincoln smiled down at her. "You have a can-do attitude. I prefer you to the man." He brought Larry closer. "Your face is asymmetrical while hers is full of optimism and life."

"Thank you, Mr. President," said Amelia. "You are a doll!"

"That's great," Larry told him. "Can you just sit down?"

The giant statue looked away. "Perhaps if you were to ask me politely."

"Would you sit down, *please*?" asked Larry.

Lincoln closed his eyes. "You didn't mean that."

Larry looked down at Amelia. "This guy is impossible. I can't deal with him."

"He's right," she said, crossing her arms. "You didn't mean it."

"Well it's hard to mean it when he says my face is asymmetrical," Larry replied.

"Mr. President, will you please sit down?" asked Amelia.

"I am doing it for you, miss," said the statue. He set Larry down beside Amelia. Then he backed into his giant stone seat. With a thick stone finger, he flicked a pigeon off his shoulder.

"These wretched beasts and their constant cooing."

Amelia tugged on Larry's sleeve. "Mr. Daley! I think they're coming!"

Larry peered out from between the columns. He spotted Ivan's soldiers marching closer. He ducked back inside.

"Mr. President! I'm going to need you to hold still now," said Amelia.

Larry and Amelia hid behind the large columns while the statue of Lincoln sat frozen in his chair. He didn't sit, staring forward as was his usual pose. Instead, he looked up at the ceiling trying to act nonchalant. Ivan's men didn't seem to notice as they passed.

Larry and Amelia poked their heads out after the men passed by. Once they were out of sight, they turned back to the giant former president.

"Thank you," Amelia told him.

"We should be okay heading to Air and Space now," said Larry.

The statue smiled at them. "If I may say so, you do make a charming twosome."

"Thank you," said Larry. "But we're not a...I mean...it's not like that."

Lincoln frowned. "I never lie! You two are perfectly adorable!" He leaned forward and peered toward the Castle. "Too bad you will probably lose. From what I can see, you are facing an invincible foe who will almost certainly vanquish you."

"Come on. What's that?" asked Larry. "Aren't you supposed to be inspirational?"

"Inspiration born of naive optimism is worthless," replied Lincoln. "However, if your cause is just, young man, you shall succeed."

Larry nodded. "Thank you."

"But it is going to be very, very hard," Lincoln quickly added.

Larry growled with frustration as they left the memorial.

The two made their way back across the dark Mall. There was no sign of Ivan's men anywhere. They were able to sneak back to the Air and Space Museum. As they neared, Larry could see outlines of the various aircraft through the large bay windows.

Amelia beamed. "I have a feeling I'm going to like this place."

Larry led her into the side entrance. "Let's just find Einstein and ask him the riddle."

When they entered the hangarlike museum, everything was the same as it was when Larry passed through earlier. The mannequins and aircraft were frozen in place, like before. However, Larry noticed the tablet begin to glow.

"Uh-oh," he said.

Suddenly, the Smithsonian Air and Space Museum came to life. One by one, wax pilots inside the cockpits began flipping switches. Engines sputtered bursts of black smoke as they revved up. Propellers spun and motors began to hum.

In the moon landing exhibit, the Neil Armstrong mannequin climbed down the ladder of the Apollo Lander. "That's one small step for mannequins," said the astronaut.

Near one of the catwalks, the Wright brothers checked the engine of their original bi-wing plane. The primitive craft hung nearby, suspended from the ceiling like many of the other planes. The brothers were the first to fly and appeared to be getting ready to do it again.

Back on the ground, two Tuskegee Airmen crossed the floor. Dressed in full flight suits, the famous pilots were the first African-American pilots of World War II.

"The Tuskegee Airmen are on the march," said the first airman. He sounded like an old newsreel announcer.

The second airman stopped and turned to him. "Can you stop narrating everything we do and just live in the moment?"

"The Tuskegee Airmen are living in the moment!" replied the first airman.

The pilots stopped in front of Larry and Amelia. "Miss Earhart," said the second airman. "I just wanted to say thanks."

"What for, Captain?" asked Amelia.

"A lot of people didn't think we could fly either," he replied. "Thanks for clearing the runway, ma'am."

The first pilot blotted a tear from his eye. "In a historic meeting, the Tuskegee Airmen officially thank Amelia Earhart for breaking gender and racial barriers in the sky!"

The captain glared back at him. "See, now why do you have to do that?" he asked. "It completely ruined the moment." He turned back to Amelia and grinned. "Race you to Paris?"

Amelia grinned. "You're on!"

She was about to dash off with the two airmen when Larry caught her arm. "Hey, hey, hey!"

"Sorry," said Amelia. She smiled sheepishly. "It's in the blood."

As they continued through the museum, Amelia stopped and smiled. "There she is, Mr. Daley." She pointed to a large red plane with a single propeller. "Old Bessie," she said with pride. "That gal took me across the Atlantic."

She strolled over to inspect her plane while Larry continued toward the gift shop. When he got there, he saw that all the Einstein dolls were missing.

"All right, Einsteins, where are you?"

Then a voice echoed throughout the museum. "Washington, you are clear for take-off. In ten...nine...eight..."

Larry froze. "Oh no."

A mission control mannequin sat at the security desk. He wore a short-sleeved shirt with a tie. He adjusted his thick-framed glasses as he counted down a rocket launch on the museum's PA system. "Seven...six...five..." The place filled with smoke as several of the rockets prepared to launch. More planes began warming up, as well.

Larry raced to the desk. He yanked the microphone from the man's hand and held it to his mouth. "Okay, we are a *no go* on the launch, people," he announced. "I repeat that's a big November Gopher on the launch." He tried to think of phrases that mission control would use. "Tower control says we have zero visibility and a ceiling of two hundred feet. Which means...we're on the highway to the danger zone." He glanced around. Everyone seemed to be buying it. "As of now, tower is grounding all nonessential craft. And essential craft, too. Stay frosty. Maverick out."

The pilots glared at Larry with disappointed expressions. Luckily, they listened to him. One by one, they shut down their engines. Even the rockets powered down.

Larry left the booth and halted in mid stride. Standing in front of him was a little capuchin monkey in a space suit. Larry knelt in front of him. "Hey, little space monkey."

The monkey pointed to the name tag on his suit. It read: Able, first monkey in space. The monkey stood at attention and gave a salute.

"Okay, Able," said Larry. He returned the salute and smiled. "At ease."

The monkey chirped happily and extended a paw. He wanted to shake hands.

"Wow, you're a polite little guy, aren't you?" He shook the monkey's paw. "Say, you wouldn't happen to know where I could find those Einstein bobble-head dolls would you?"

The monkey nodded and pointed over Larry's shoulder. Unfortunately, when Larry turned to look, the monkey snatched the tablet. He dashed away, chirping in a way that sounded suspiciously like laughter.

"No!" yelled Larry. He scrambled after him. "Bad space monkey!"

Able scurried to the moon landing exhibit. He climbed over the short plastic barrier surrounding the display. He climbed up the moon lander and chattered tauntingly. Larry gave chase, leaping over the barrier. However, once he was over the fake moon surface, he began to float higher and higher, as if he were really on the real moon. Somersaulting, he floated over Able's head.

As Larry slowly came down, Able pushed off the lander. Larry lunged for him as they passed each other. "Come on!" he shouted. "I don't have a good vertical reach!"

The monkey chattered happily as they continued to bounce past each other. "I know you think this is fun," Larry growled. "But it's not!"

Able seemed to disagree as they bounded past each other again.

Finally, Larry reached out and gripped the edge of the tablet. Able held tight and the two spun through the air. As they rotated, they spun away from the display. Once they passed over the barrier, the low gravity effect vanished. Regular gravity took over and they both came crashing to the ground. Larry lost his grip on the tablet.

"Okay, I see I'm not getting through to you," said Larry. "I'm going to try to put this in terms you understand."

Larry crouched in front of the monkey and began to chirp and make hand signals. His chatter sounded just like Able's. He politely asked for the tablet.

The monkey's eyes widened. He made hand signals back at Larry. "*Where did you learn Capuchin?*" asked Able.

"*A friend of mine in New York taught me,*" Larry replied with grunts and more hand gestures. "*I know. It's a lot to take in.*"

"*I have a brother in New York,*" said Able. "*Unfortunately, we are estranged.*"

"*I like you, space monkey,*" said Larry. "*When you want something you stick to it. It reminds me of myself. There's only a two percent difference in our DNA. But right now it feels more like one.*"

Able looked down at the tablet then up at Larry. He gave a final chirp then handed it back.

"*Attaboy,*" said Larry. "*Friends?*"

The monkey gave him a hug.

CHAPTER 7

While Kahmunrah waited for his minions to capture Larry Daley, he found other ways to occupy his time. He began by pilfering several other exhibits in the museum. He piled the artifacts around the Door to the Underworld and reveled in his newfound treasures. Unfortunately, not all his new possessions were valuable. He quickly discovered that Dorothy's ruby slippers from the *Wizard of Oz* movie weren't even made of real rubies.

However, he was rather pleased with the satin robe he had just found. It used to belong to a famous boxer named Muhammad Ali. The athlete was famous for saying he could "float like a butterfly and sting like a bee."

"You know what?" asked Kahmunrah as he modeled the robe. "I do feel like a butterfly."

Ivan the Terrible interrupted his personal fashion show. "These two heard we were taking over the world and they want in." The Russian jutted his thumb over his shoulder. "Their names are Darth Vader and Oscar the Grouch. They claim to be on display here, too."

Waiting just off to the side was a tall man wearing a black cape, a black mask, and a black helmet. He seemed to have some sort of breathing problem.

The other creature was much shorter. He was green and fuzzy, with a huge mouth and big white eyes. And he was in a metal trash can. The two were the strangest things the pharaoh had ever seen.

"I don't know who they are," said Kahmunrah. "I don't even know *what* they are." He waved them off. "My axis of evil is full. Thanks anyway. Bye now."

"Ah, come on," said the short green one. "I'm good with letters and numbers, if you need somebody in that department."

"I don't need you," said the pharaoh. "You don't even seem that evil. Just vaguely...grouchy."

The one called Darth Vader held out a hand and made a choking motion. His hand trembled and his breathing increased. He seemed to be putting a lot of effort into the act.

"What are you doing?" asked Kahmunrah. He made the gesture back to the man in black. "Ooh, scary hand gesture. What does that even mean?"

The masked figure dropped his hand and hung his head. He picked up Oscar's trash can and they left the gallery.

"I've found them!" announced Napoléon. He peered through a long brass telescope at the front window.

Kahmunrah dashed to the window and took the telescope. He gazed across to the Air and Space Museum. Through its many windows he saw displays alive and moving. He also caught a glimpse of a pitiful little man in a dark blue uniform—Larry Daley.

He pushed the telescope back to Napoléon. "Go! All of you!" he ordered. "To Air and Space! Gather your men! Bring me the tablet and the combination. Whatever it takes!"

Ivan, Napoléon, and their men grabbed their weapons and scrambled for the exit. Only Al Capone stayed behind. A wide grin spread across his face. "So, does that mean..."

"Yes, Mr. Capone," replied Kahmunrah. "*Now*, it's killing time."

From her cramped position, Sacajawea couldn't see through the slightly opened container doors. Luckily, Dexter crouched beside the tiny rust hole. He chirped quietly as they heard footsteps approaching.

"All right, fellas," said a voice outside. It was Al Capone. "Looks like Valentine's Day came early this year. Let's go have some fun!"

As the footsteps faded away, Dexter screeched excitedly. He turned to the Neanderthals and chattered. One of the hairy cavemen relayed the message to the Huns through a series of grunts and hand gestures.

Attila turned to Sacajawea. "*Ooga. Musha-toombra*," he said.

She relayed the message to General Custer. "The guards have abandoned their post."

"Excellent!" said the general. He twirled the tip of his mustache. "You know, I have thought long and hard about what you said. Now, I have a new and improved battle strategy." He huddled close. "I will loudly announce that we are *not* going to attack." He nodded and grinned. "And then...wait for it...tension grows...and then...we *will* attack! Any questions?"

"Here's one," said Sacajawea. "Didn't you lose very badly at Little Bighorn?"

"Okay, first of all, stuff happens," said Custer. He rolled his eyes. "The liberal media blew that way out of proportion. The fact is, I had some bad intel. And honestly, if I had to do it over again, I'd do it exactly the same way! Two words...mission accomplished!"

Sacajawea sighed as she pushed past him. She opened the door and stepped out of the container.

"I have your Einsteins!" yelled Amelia.

Larry spun around, following her voice. He wove through the busy crowd of pilots and astronauts, making his way to the information desk. There, he saw a dozen little Einstein dolls gathered around several scraps of papers. Some lay on their stomachs pointing to the pages while others scribbled equations and formulas. They bickered and discussed several scientific theories that were way over Larry's head.

"Uh, Mr. Einstein…s?" he said. They looked up in unison.

Amelia pointed to the tablet in Larry's hands. "Gentlemen. We're trying to crack the combination to this doodad," she explained. "And the writing here says we'll find it if we figure out the heart of pharaoh's tomb."

One of the Einsteins laughed. "That's an easy one! Don't you get it, kid? It's a riddle!"

Larry rolled his eyes. "A riddle? I hate riddles. They're boring and they make me feel dumb."

"Riddle me this, kiddo," said another Einstein. "How many words can you make from the letters of the word *tablet*?"

"I just told you that I don't like riddles," said Larry.

"Tablet, tab, battle," rattled off another Einstein.

"Latte, beta," added another.

Yet another joined in. "Belt, bleat."

"Wait. Stop it!" said Larry.

"Fifty six!" shouted the first Einstein. "If you include tablet!"

One of the Einsteins tapped the tablet. "The answer is in the question, you see," he explained. "*Figure* out the secret at the *heart* of pharaoh's *tomb*."

"*Saying* it with *emphasis* on every other *word* doesn't help me," Larry mocked.

The little doll shook his bobbly head. "*Figure* out," he said. "It's a figure. You know, a number."

"And the part about the pharaoh's tomb," added another doll. "That means the pyramids."

"Don't you get it, kid?" asked yet another Einstein. "You're looking for the secret number at the heart of the pyramids."

"Well, whistle me Dixie!" said Amelia. "The answer is pi!"

Larry shook his head. "What?"

Amelia explained, "3.14, you know, the ratio between any circle's circumference to its diameter."

Larry wished he'd paid more attention in math class.

"It's 3.14159265, to be exact," corrected the first Einstein. "The Egyptian's knew all about pi."

"Also, if the circumference of a pyramid is divided by twice its height, you get pi," explained the tiny bobble-head. "The internal chamber, in cubits, always measures pi. That's your combination kid,—3.14159265."

"Wow. Thanks," said Larry. He tried to memorize the number. "Okay, 3.14...2..."

"It's 3.14159265," corrected the little Albert Einstein.

Larry said, "3.14956..."

"No," said the Einstein, "3.14159265."

Amelia grabbed Larry's arm. "I got it," she said, pulling him away from the information desk. They ran across the museum floor. "So, what's our next move, partner?"

Larry checked his watch. "We have about seven minutes to get out of here and get back to Jed." He smiled at her. "Thanks for your help with the whole pi thing."

"We make a pretty good team," said Amelia. She smiled back at him. "Perhaps *more* than a team?"

Larry stopped running. "Okay, wait. What do you want me to say?" he asked. "Do I think you're one of the coolest women I've ever met?

Absolutely! Are you also mind-numbingly gorgeous?" He nodded. "Yes, you are! But where does this leave us? Because, trust me, there are some major long-term compatibility issues here."

"Well thank you very much, Mr. Daley," she said with a smile. "And ditto, by the way. But now we have *six* minutes to save your Lilliputian lassoer." She held out a hand. "Shall we?"

Larry smiled and took her hand. He led the way as they ran across the museum floor. He headed straight for the moon landing display.

"How do you expect for us to get over there in time?" asked Amelia.

Larry pointed to the two-seater vehicle on the fake moon surface. It looked like a giant go-cart covered in tinfoil. "I was thinking we'd take the Moon Rover."

Amelia ground to a halt. "That's a cockamamie idea if I ever heard one," she said. "Your cowboy friend will be in a Saharan sarcophagus by the time we get there. I have a better idea." She tried to pull him away.

Larry held fast. "No, I think the rover is pretty much the way to go."

"Mr. Daley, why are you avoiding the obvious?" She waved a hand at all the hanging airplanes.

Larry shook his head. "I don't know what you're talking about." Although he knew exactly what she was talking about.

She grinned and cocked her head. "Are you afraid to fly, Mr. Daley?"

"No," he replied.

"Well, then what is it?" she asked. "Why the midair stall?"

"I'm not stalling." He pulled her back toward the moon display. "I just think the rover suits our needs."

This time Amelia held fast. "You *are* afraid to fly, aren't you?"

"No," he replied. "I'm just afraid to fly...with you."

Amelia's jaw dropped. "Me? I'm one of the most famous pilots in the history of aviation."

"Yeah. Famous for getting lost," said Larry. He gave a long sigh. "I'm sorry, but it's true."

Amelia placed both hands on her hips. "Mr. Daley, I assure you I have *never* been lost a day in my life. I may not have always been on course.

But I was always where I belonged." She pointed to a nearby airplane. "In that cockpit, with blue sky all around. Doing what I loved." She poked a finger at his chest. "It seems to me, Mr. Daley, that if anyone here has gotten *lost*, it's you."

Ding!

The nearby elevator doors opened. Al Capone, Napoléon Bonaparte, Ivan the Terrible, and their men poured out. Capone was the first to spot them. He raised his tommy-gun, cocked it, and leveled it at Larry and Amelia. "Time for me to paint the town red!" he shouted.

Larry cringed as Capone pulled the trigger. However, he only pretended to spray them with bullets. Fortunately for Larry and Amelia, the machine gun was only a prop. Nevertheless, the gun rocked in the gangster's hands as he pretended to mow them down—in slow motion.

Napoléon tapped him on the shoulder. "What are you doing?"

"Taking them down, gangster style!" replied Capone through gritted teeth.

"But you're not doing anything," said Ivan. "You're just *pretending* to do something...very slowly."

The gangster kept firing. "You don't get it. This is how we gangsters do it," he explained. He made little machine-gun noises with his mouth as he pretended to shoot. "Tch-tch-tch-tch! Bullet, bullet, bullet! Public enemy number one, baby!"

Ivan and Napoléon looked at each other and shook their heads. Then they took off toward Larry and Amelia.

"No time for your rover now, Mr. Daley!" said Amelia. She grabbed his hand and they ran up the nearby stairs leading to a catwalk. The hoard of bad guys sprinted after them. When they reached the top, Amelia pointed to a nearby airplane. She shrugged her shoulders. "It'll have to do."

She hadn't only pointed to an airplane, she pointed to the very *first* airplane—the 1903 Wright Flyer. Orville and Wilbur Wright were on a platform on the other side. They seemed to be going over some blueprints for the next model.

"No, no, no, no, no!" said Larry. "That's the first plane ever made! It's not even a real plane. It's made out of balsa wood and paper!"

She pulled him closer. "It's made out of spruce and canvas and good old-fashioned American ingenuity," she said. They reached the plane and she flung a leg over the railing. "Mr. Daley, are you coming or what?" She stepped out onto the wing.

Larry looked back to see the Kamunrah's allies closing in. Meanwhile, an engine coughed to life behind him. Amelia was lying down at the front of the Flyer, the propellers beginning to spin.

"Well? Hop on, slowpoke," she said.

Larry turned back to the bad guys. Maybe they could make it to another airplane. After all, if they had to escape by plane, perhaps they could make use of a more advanced craft—meaning...anything else in the museum.

Napoléon, Capone, Ivan, and their men neared the bottom of the stairs. He and Amelia wouldn't be going back that way. Luckily, the two Tuskegee Airmen blocked their way.

"Sorry, gentlemen." One of the airmen held out a hand. "But this bird is flying the coop."

"Out of our way!" ordered Ivan the Terrible.

The airman who enjoyed speaking like a news commentator leaned forward. "And in bold confrontation, the famed Tuskegee Airmen face off against Ivan the Terrible, Napoléon, and Al Capone!" he said. "Things just got weird, folks!"

Larry didn't have any other choice but to board the Wright Flyer. He threw a leg over the railing and carefully walked along one of its wings. Once he was in the cockpit, if he could call it that, he lay down beside Amelia. She revved the engine and the plane moved forward, pulling against its cables.

The Wright brothers dropped their plans and spun toward their plane. "A woman can't fly a plane!" yelled Wilbur Wright.

"Think again, boys!" said Amelia.

Orville turned to Wilbur. "Mom is going to kill us if anything happens to that thing."

As the engine revved higher, the cables snapped. The plane tipped forward, then soared away from the platform. Larry held tight as the Flyer buzzed over Capone and the others. All the bad guys hit the deck. The Tuskegee Airmen stood at attention and gave the Flyer a salute.

"Thanks, fellas!" said Amelia. She grinned as she piloted the Flyer through the huge museum.

They soared under other suspended planes and banked around rockets and space capsules. Larry was glad he hadn't eaten anything recently.

Suddenly, they banked sharply to the left. "Uh-oh!" said Amelia.

"What?" asked Larry. "I don't like to hear *uh-oh* on an airplane!"

Amelia struggled with the Flyer's control stick. "Just a slight wrinkle, Mr. Daley! We have a cantankerous cable in the cockpit."

"What?" asked Larry.

"One of the wires is jammed," she explained. "I'm going to have to loosen it! Take the stick!" She let go of the stick and began to scoot backward.

"What? No!" said Larry.

"I know you've got moxie in you yet!" said Amelia. She turned and tugged on one of the many cables running to the back of the craft.

Larry had no choice but to grab the stick. "Moxie doesn't fly planes," he said. "People with pilot licenses fly planes!"

Larry's hands shook as he clutched the stick. While Amelia struggled with the cable, Larry flew the plane through the museum. Sweat formed on his forehead as they darted around the suspended planes. He steered the plane as best he could around more huge displays.

The plane banked to the right, heading into a wide-open space. Luckily, Larry didn't have to dodge any more hanging aircraft. Unluckily, they zoomed toward the large bay doors the museum used to bring in the large planes. Even more unluckily, the doors were closed.

Larry glanced down and spotted the little space monkey. "Able, the doors!" he shouted.

Able saluted and then sprung into action. He hopped over exhibits and swung from the railings. He made his way to the far wall and slammed his paw onto a big red button. The bottom doors slowly opened.

"Got it!" yelled Amelia as she pulled the cable free. The stick bucked in Larry's hand as the plane dove for the floor. Amelia crawled back to the front. "We're flat-hatting when we should be in an adverse yaw!" she shouted.

"Those are words I don't understand!" yelled Larry.

Amelia put her hands over Larry's. "Pull up!" she ordered.

Together, they pulled the stick back. The plane skimmed the floor just before climbing higher. It shot through the open doors and into the night sky. The cool air ruffled Larry's hair as they flew over the Mall.

Don't worry, Jed, Larry thought. *I'm coming!*

CHAPTER 8

*C*RAAAAASH!

The Castle's stained-glass window shattered as the Wright Flyer crashed through. Larry held tight as the plane lunged toward Kahmunrah. The pharaoh dove for cover as the Flyer slammed to the ground and skidded across the floor. Thrown free, Larry tumbled end over end. Amelia stayed with the craft as it kept sliding. It crashed through several displays at the other end of the commons. When it finally stopped, it was buried under a pile of debris.

Larry got to his feet. He couldn't see Amelia. He started toward the wreck to see if she was all right.

"Stop!" Kahmunrah ordered. He held Jed's hourglass high over his head as if he were going to smash it to the ground. "Nice entrance, Mr. Daley. Surely you could have figured out a way to create more damage." He gave the hourglass a shake. Larry saw that Jed was buried chest deep in sand. "Speaking of which, I hope for your little friend's sake that you figured out the combination."

Larry held out a hand. "First, give me Jed."

"Right after you give me the combination." The pharaoh smiled. "And the tablet, of course."

"Release my friends *and* give me Jed," Larry bargained. "And I'll give you the tablet *and* the combination."

Kahmunrah sighed. "I'll release what I want to release when I want to release it." He clenched his teeth. "Now, give me the tablet *and* the combination right now or I shall kill *all* your friends, starting with the little shaggy-haired cowman here!"

Larry nodded. "All right. How about I give you the tablet as you're giving me Jed?"

The pharaoh frowned. "Mr. Daley."

"Then you release my friends *while* I'm giving you the combination," Larry added.

"Mr. Daley," Kahmunrah repeated.

"Come on, that's fair," Larry explained. "That way we're both giving and getting at the same time."

"Mr. Daley!" the pharaoh roared. "My patience is wearing extraordinarily thin! Now, I'm giving you exactly five seconds to give me what I want!"

"We already got the combination," said a voice from behind.

Larry turned to see Al Capone stroll through the front door. The rest of his goons followed, along with the other villains from history.

"It's pi," said Capone. The young gangster held up a tiny Einstein bobble-head statue. "It's 3.14159265. Crazy hair here sang like a canary."

Capone chuckled and tossed Einstein to the ground. He skidded to a stop at Larry's feet. "I'm sorry, Larry," said the little doll. "But in the timeless struggle between brain and brawn, I'm afraid...brawn always wins."

The goons surrounded Larry. Kahmunrah marched forward and snatched the tablet from his hands. "Must be a real bummer, Mr. Daley, to know that all your valiant efforts were, in the end, for naught."

He turned and casually tossed the hourglass over his shoulder. Larry lunged forward, catching it at the last second. He flipped it over so Jed no longer was being buried in sand.

The pharaoh marched toward the Door to the Underworld. "What a terrible disappointment you must be to yourself." He plugged the golden tablet into the door and entered the code. The tablet began to glow, and a loud hum filled the room. Kahmunrah grinned and held a hand to his ear. "Do you know what sound that is?" he asked. "That's the sound of *The End!*"

Larry looked down at the cowboy in the hourglass. "I'm sorry, Jed."

"Hey, you tried, Gigantor," Jedediah replied. "We almost had him, too."

"No, I'm sorry I wasn't there, the last couple years, at the museum," Larry explained. "Maybe none of this would have happened."

"Hey," said Jedediah. "You're here now."

Larry sighed. "Lot of help that did you."

"Don't you get it?" asked Jedediah. "I didn't call you because we needed you. I mean, sure, we were in a pickle. But it wouldn't be the first time we had to wrestle our way out of a root sack." He stared Larry in the eyes. "No, partner. I called because *you* needed *us*. That fancy suit you been parading around these past couple years? That ain't you."

Larry knew Jedediah was right. Even though he had fought for his and his friends' lives the entire night, Larry had never felt so alive. All the new products, sales numbers, and business meetings couldn't give him the satisfaction he had as a night guard. The uniform wasn't so fancy, the pay was lousy, and the hours were terrible. But being a night guard had been the best job he ever had.

KRA-VOOM!

The museum shook beneath his feet. The tablet grew brighter as each of the squares began to rotate. They spun faster and faster, then stopped one by one, like the wheels of a slot machine. Everyone shielded his eyes as the tablet flashed bright like the sun.

With a menacing rumble, the Door to the Underworld opened slowly. Even though the stone door was attached to a freestanding wall, its magic let it open to another dimension. Smoked billowed out of the darkness beyond as moans and tormented cries could be heard in the distance.

The pharaoh turned to face everyone. "Welcome to the new extended reign of Kahmunrah!" He raised his hands high. "Fifth king of Egypt, and now...the world!"

The head of a giant hawk peeked out of the darkness. It squawked loudly before stepping forward. Although the creature had the head of a hawk, it had a huge man's body. It wore golden armor and held a long sharp spear. A similar beast marched through behind it. Its hawk head twitched back and forth, taking in its new surroundings. It then focused its beady black eyes on Larry and screeched. Eight more beasts poured through the darkened doorway.

"Horus. My warriors," said Kahmunrah. He pointed to Larry. "Send Larry Daley and his friends to their doom."

Larry grasped the hourglass tightly and stepped backward. The hawk-headed giants leveled their spears and closed in. Their sharp beaks snapped open and shut as if ready to tear into him. Soon, Larry and Jedediah were surrounded by razor sharp spearheads.

"*Mak, keter om,*" Kahmunrah boomed. "*Om neter kah!*"

The creatures raised their spears, ready to strike. Larry shut his eyes tight.

"Hold!" shouted a voice.

Larry opened one eye and peered at the museum's front door. Everyone else, including the Horus, turned to see who spoke. However, the doorway was empty.

"The mighty Octavius has returned!" said the tiny voice from the doorway. "Do you wish to surrender honorably, Kahmunrah?" Octavius rode into view. "Or must this end with the spilling of your blood?"

The tiny Roman commander sat atop a reddish brown squirrel. The small rodent twitched his bushy tail and glanced around. Octavius nudged the squirrel's sides with his heels and the creature scampered closer.

Kahmunrah laughed. "This?" He pointed to the squirrel. "*This* is your big rescue?"

Octavius grinned. "No. *This* is." He pointed to the shattered window.

The sound of breaking glass filled the room as a huge marble hand knocked away the rest of the crumbling panes. Everyone gasped as the giant Abraham Lincoln statue stepped inside. Even the Horus stepped back and raised their spears at the new threat.

Octavius looked up at Jed. "I brought help," he shouted. "Big help, as was my charge."

"I knew you would, partner!" Jed yelled back.

"What *is* that...thing?" asked Kahmunrah.

Lincoln scowled. "I am no thing." He pointed down at the pharaoh. "And why are you wearing a dress?"

"It's a tunic," Kahmunrah barked, stamping a foot. Then he turned to the stunned Horus warriors. "What are you waiting for? Attack it!"

The creatures rushed toward Lincoln. They threw their spears but the sharp weapons merely bounced off his marble chest. The huge president reached down and swiped them aside with one hand. "Disgusting half-pigeons!" he said, scowling.

Seeing no way to defeat the giant, the hawk men ran back through the Door to the Underworld. Those who still had spears dropped them as they made their retreat. Once all were through, the door slammed shut with a loud *BOOM!*

Kahmunrah threw up his hands in disgust. "Well, that's just...fabulous." He stared at Larry. "I shall, however, find some consolation in watching you die, Larry Daley." He turned to Capone and his men. "Kill him now," he ordered.

Before the gangsters could make a move, a bugle sounded. Larry turned to see a welcome sight. Amelia Earhart walked side by side with the Tuskegee Airmen and General Custer atop his horse. The rest of the mannequins from New York marched behind them. Sacajawea, the Huns, and the cavemen were joined by The Thinker and the flying cupids. Behind them were columns of tiny Roman soldiers and a stampede of little cowboys. In the very back, the giant squid slithered forward, bringing up the rear.

General Custer raised his saber. He glanced around, took a deep breath, and shouted, "We are *not* going to attack right now!" With that, the entire group charged.

The pharaoh gave Napoléon and one of his soldiers a shove forward. "Don't just stand there. Get them!"

The two sides clashed like great armies have for centuries. Except this battle was like none seen in history. Huns fought with gangsters, Russians clashed with cavemen, and French soldiers battled ancient statues. Larry had seen a lot of strange things in his time as a night guard, but this was, by far, the strangest.

"It appears my work here is done," said Lincoln. He turned back to the window.

"Hey, where are you going?" asked Larry. "We need you."

"You'll be fine now," Lincoln reassured. "Just remember, son...a house divided cannot stand." A wide grin spread across the marble man's face. "I have come to like you despite your small frame and asymmetrical face. You'll be fine now. I've given you what you need." He started toward the window then stopped and bent down. He picked up a penny from the ground. "Hey, look! That's me! I'm on money!"

As Lincoln ambled into the night, Larry turned back to the battle. It was fortunate that he did. He ducked as a Russian warrior swung a mace at his head. The metal club just missed his scalp but knocked the hourglass out of his hands. Jedediah bounced around the glass container as it tumbled across the floor. It came to a stop a few feet away, resting upright. Once again, Jed was being buried in sand.

CHAPTER 9

"Forward, mighty steed!" Octavius ordered.

He gave a kick and the squirrel reared up and chattered loudly. It sprung forward and scampered toward the fallen hourglass. They zigzagged around the shuffling feet of the fighting mannequins.

When they reached the hourglass, Octavius leaped off the squirrel and put a hand on the glass. "Do you hear that?" he asked. "They need us!"

Jedediah struggled against the falling sand. It was up to his chin. "Sorry, but I think this cowboy has seen his last hoedown." He sighed and gazed off into the distance. "I'm nothing more than a tiny hill of beans in this great big land of ours."

Octavius smiled and took off his helmet. "No need for final words, my friend."

Jedediah looked disappointed. "But I have a whole speech planned," he explained. "It's both manly *and* touching."

Octavius shook his head. "No, because you are going to live."

The Roman reared back and smashed his helmet against the glass. The hourglass shattered and sand poured out. Jedediah tumbled out along with it. Octavius helped the cowboy to his feet.

Jedediah smiled. "Thanks, partner." He poured the sand out of his hat and put it on.

They climbed back onto the squirrel. Octavius drew his sword and handed it to Jedediah. One of Octavius's soldiers tossed him another.

Jed slapped the Roman on the back. "Let's go to work."

The commander kicked the squirrel's sides and it sprang forward. As they dashed back into the fray, the two tiny warriors jabbed at the enemy's ankles.

Seeing Jed was safe, Larry made his way toward the Door to the Underworld. He stayed low, dodging stabbing spears, thrusting bayonets, and swinging clubs. He glanced up and locked eyes with Amelia at the other side of the small battlefield. He pointed toward the tablet still locked in the ancient door. She nodded and they both moved toward it.

Larry dove for cover just as one of Napoléon's soldiers jabbed at him with a bayonet. He ducked behind a display case and found he wasn't alone. General Custer shivered as he sat with his knees drawn up to his chest.

"What are you doing?" asked Larry.

Custer jumped at the sound of Larry's voice. "Hiding," he replied.

"What?" asked Larry. "We need you!"

Custer closed his eyes and shook his head. "Oh, I'm a failure."

"Come on," said Larry. "Everyone feels that way sometimes."

The general gazed up at him with wide eyes. "Did *you* foolishly lead two-hundred and eight Americans to their doom at Little Big Horn?"

"Well...no," replied Larry.

Custer clutched his knees tighter. "Not good. Not good at all."

Larry nodded. "Yeah, no way to get around that one."

"I mean, that is a confidence killer, man!" Custer explained. "I blew it. I mean...I blew it big time. Sure, I talk a good game." He looked down at his shoulder. "Maybe I don't deserve these stripes anymore. I'll always be famous for my biggest failure!"

Larry poked his head out from behind the case. Kahmunrah's men were winning the fight. After all, the pharaoh had enlisted three great military leaders from history. They were organized and easily pushed back Larry's friends—who needed a great leader on *their* side.

Larry grabbed Custer by the arms and gave him a shake. "Hey, look," he said. "Little Big Horn, all that? That's history. Literally." He pointed to the nearby battle. "Right here, this place, this night. *This* is what they'll remember you for." He stared the general in the eyes. "*This* is your Last Stand."

Custer's face softened and the familiar gleam returned to his eyes. He smirked, took a deep breath, and drew his saber.

"You ready to do this?" asked Larry.

Custer nodded. "Ready."

The two climbed out from behind the case and marched into the melee. "All right, listen up, troops!" barked Custer. "The moon is full, and that means the tide is about to turn!" He pointed toward the squid. "Daddy long legs, you're taking up too much space! We don't need you! Pull back!"

The squid began to slide backward, but Larry crouched beside it. "Squid, we *totally* need you!" he said. "You have reach on them. Make those extras arms count!" As the squid slid toward the enemy, Larry ran to catch up with the general.

Custer pointed up at the cherubs. "Naked babies, lull them into complacency with your beautiful song."

Larry came along behind him. "No, you have arrows," Larry corrected. "Shoot people!"

The cupids nodded and whipped out their tiny bows and arrows. They flew toward the enemy. Larry caught up with Custer near The Thinker.

The general picked up a drum and tossed it to the statue. "Iron man, beat this drum in a steady military fashion!"

Larry came behind him and took the drum from the statue. "Don't do that at all! It's a complete waste of time!" He slapped the bronze statue on the back. "Thinker, you're my muscle! Get in there! Mix it up!"

Custer climbed onto his horse and gave Larry a salute. "Thank you for following my lead," he said with a grin.

"Anytime, General," said Larry.

As Larry made his way through the battle, he could see the tide turning. The squid slapped away Capone's gangsters while The Thinker knocked out several French soldiers with one blow.

Sacajawea continued to fire her bow and arrow at the enemy until she was surrounded by Russian troops. Luckily, the cherub statues flew by, pelting Ivan's men with tiny stone arrows. They couldn't help but sing a victory song:

We're flying like sparrows,
Shooting our arrows,
And they're quite harmful,
They're made of marble.

Even Jed and Octavius continued to assault bad guys with their stabs to the ankles. Once the enemy looked down, the Huns and the cavemen swooped in to finish the job.

As Larry worked his way through the chaos, he stopped when he saw a tiny monkey in a space suit. "Able, what're you doing here?"

The monkey replied in a series of chirps and hand gestures. "*I wanted to help in the glorious resistance,*" said the monkey.

Larry heard more monkey chatter behind him. He spun around to see Dexter scampering up.

"*Able?*" Dexter asked in Capuchin.

"*Dexter?*" asked Able.

"*You guys know each other?*" asked Larry.

Dexter screeched his reply. "*Indeed, we are brothers. But we are estranged. Ever since he went into space and decided he was too good for the family.*"

"*You have never gotten over living in my shadow, banana breath,*" screeched Able.

"*That is unkind,*" squawked Dexter.

Larry knelt between them. "*This really isn't the time to get into this.*"

Just then, both monkeys tried to slap each other. They ended up slapping Larry in the face instead. "Hey!" he shouted, slapping them back. Both monkeys slapped Larry again, harder.

"*Okay, stop! Stop!*" Larry held up his hands. "*I know you guys understand me! You are both proud capuchins! Whether in space or in the jungle, brothers you are.*" He pointed to the nearby battle. "*Now how about we focus on slapping the enemy.*"

The monkeys looked at each other, then back at Larry. They each grinned widely and then took off into the fray. Attila had just knocked down one of Capone's men. The monkeys hopped onto the thug's chest and began to slap him silly.

Larry hurried to the door to find Amelia huddling nearby. "Are you all right?" he asked.

Amelia smiled. "Never better!"

Larry reached up and snatched the tablet from the door. "Okay, when I give you the signal, open the door."

"How will I do that?" she asked.

"Don't worry," he replied. "You'll know."

Amelia grinned. "I take it you have a plan?"

Larry smirked and nodded. "It's time to divide the house."

He stood and marched toward Ivan, Napoléon, and Capone. The three leaders stood behind the battle, barking orders at their men. When Larry approached, they all pointed weapons at him.

Ivan the Terrible glanced at the tablet. He held out a hand. "The tablet. Now."

"What do you want that thing for?" asked Capone. "We just saw that the birdy army is a bust."

"I have developed a taste for this...coming to life," Ivan replied. "Without the tablet, *nyet*. No more alive."

Napoléon and Capone's eyes widened in understanding. They nodded at each other and joined Ivan as he moved in on Larry.

"Okay," said Larry. "You guys win. Just tell me who's in charge and I'll hand it over." He chuckled. "Or should I just give it to Kahmunrah. You know, your *master*."

The three glanced at each other. "*Nyet!*" barked Ivan. "He is not our master!"

"He's not?" asked Larry. He allowed himself another chuckle. "All right, if that's what you say. It looks like he is to me, though." He shrugged. "So, I'll just give it to the boss of you three. Who would that be? Which one of you is the boss?"

All three reached out at once. Ivan quickly slapped away Capone's hand. "This man is a peasant! I am the only one among us of noble blood!"

Capone snarled at the Russian. Larry decided to stir the pot some more. "Yeah, but Napoléon has more medals and a bigger hat."

Capone slapped away Napoléon's hand. "You may have medals, but if you put your little child's hands on that tablet, it'll be the last thing those teeny mitts ever touch!"

Capone reached out but Napoléon slapped his hand away. The gangster slapped Napoléon's hand in return. Soon, the two were engaged in a slapping frenzy bigger than Able and Dexter's.

Then Capone shoved Napoléon into Ivan. The Russian trembled with rage. "I am Ivan the Terrible! That's right, I've decided to embrace my terribleness since the nuances of my historical legacy seem wasted anyway!"

He lunged at the other two, knocking them to the ground. Soon, all three were wrestling around like kids in a school yard.

Larry crossed his arms and laughed at the ridiculous sight. His plan had worked perfectly, and he was quite proud of himself. All of that stopped, however, when he felt something very sharp at his lower back. He turned to face Kahmunrah. The pharaoh held a long sword in his hand.

"Very clever," praised Kahmunrah. "Getting them to fight amongst themselves."

Larry backed away. "Yeah, I can't really take credit," he said. "It was really Lincoln's idea."

"Yes, well, you should've saved yourself when you had the chance," said Kahmunrah. He raised the sword high. "At least now I'll have the pleasure of killing you myself!"

Just as the pharaoh struck, Larry whipped out his flashlight. The blade clashed against the metal shaft as Larry blocked the attack. He wielded the flashlight like a sword of his own as he fought the pharaoh. The Egyptian snarled as he continued to slice at Larry. Luckily, the former night guard parried each blow easily.

Larry glanced just over Kahmunrah's shoulder. He saw Amelia creep out from behind the stone wall. He blocked another blow and spun around, tossing the tablet to her. She placed it back into the slot. Larry took the upper hand as she entered the secret code. Larry backed the pharaoh closer and closer to the door as it rumbled open.

Finally, with three quick strokes, Larry knocked the sword from the pharaoh's hand. He looked at Larry with wide eyes. "What are you?" asked Kahmunrah.

Larry holstered his flashlight. "I'm the Night Guard." Then he reared back and kicked the pharaoh in the chest. Kahmunrah flew back through the doorway.

"Noooooooooo!" yelled Kahmunrah as he disappeared into the darkness.

Larry rushed forward and pushed the door shut. Then he quickly removed the tablet.

Amelia placed her hands on her hips. "If I didn't know better, Mr. Daley, I'd say someone has found his moxie."

Larry smiled back at her, then he surveyed the scene. The battle was winding down with the good guys winning. Napoléon, Ivan, and Capone continued to wrestle while their men were on the run. Meanwhile, Larry's friends, old and new, were helping each other up and dusting themselves off.

General Custer rode over. "The Battle of the Smithsonian," he said proudly. "Perhaps the greatest battle the world will *never* know."

Larry nodded at the general "We'll know."

The cherubs flew overhead, playing a victory song. The rest of Larry's friends gathered to listen. Larry applauded. "Now you got it. Your best performance yet."

He caught a glimpse of his watch. It was almost five in the morning. "Oh, man," he said. "Sunrise is coming. I have to get you all back to the museum."

Jedediah and Octavius climbed off the squirrel. Jed looked up at Larry. "But they don't want us there anymore, Gigantor."

157

Larry knelt in front of them. "Well, *I* do." He stood and smiled at Amelia. "Miss Earhart, do you think you could hook us up with a ride?"

She smiled back. "With pleasure."

CHAPTER 10

Larry stared out of the window of Amelia's airplane, Old Bessie. The red plane banked left as they soared out of the Air and Space Museum. Below, Larry's newest friends from the Smithsonian stood in the doorway, waving good-bye.

He looked back to see all his New York friends gaze out the window as they soared over the National Mall. Sacajawea, the Huns, the Neanderthals, and Dexter stared in awe at the landscape below. Attila, however, seemed as if he might be a little airsick.

Sitting in the copilot's seat, Larry looked over at Amelia. She was more alive than ever. Just as she told him before, she was right where she belonged—in the pilot's seat.

The plane circled the Mall one last time before heading back to New York. Larry even caught a glimpse of Abraham Lincoln as they left. The giant marble statue smiled and waved good-bye.

With the ease of having a private plane, the trip seemed to take no time at all. Before he knew it, they were flying over New York City. Amelia kept the plane steady as they came in for a landing right onto Central Park West. They caught a break and the street was mostly deserted.

As the plane slowed to a stop in front of the museum, Larry hopped out. He opened the rear hatch and ushered out their passengers.

"Okay, everybody. Remember to stay with your buddy," he instructed.

When Dexter hopped down, Larry handed him the tablet. "Dex, give this back to Ahkmenrah," he ordered. "And I think you owe him an apology." The monkey chirped and scampered toward the museum.

Larry helped Sacajawea out of the plane. "Sack, get everybody down to the basement." She nodded and led the Huns and Neanderthals up the steps.

Amelia joined Larry as they watched the group enter the museum. "Well, you're back where you belong."

Larry looked up at the giant building and smiled. "Yeah, I think so."

She sighed. "I guess I should be going."

Larry took a step forward. "Look, Amelia, what I was trying to tell you earlier tonight." He rubbed the back of his neck. "I mean...there's no easy way to say this, but...come morning..."

She put a finger to his lips. "I know what's coming, Mr. Daley. I've known all along." She took a deep breath. "But it doesn't matter. You've given me the adventure of a lifetime, in one night!" She looked to the glowing eastern sky. "And I have a feeling it's going to be a beautiful sunrise." She leaned in and gave him a hug. Then she whispered into his ear. "Remember, have fun."

She pulled away, then flung her scarf over her shoulder as she turned to go. Larry caught her arm. "Amelia," he said, pulling her close. Then he kissed her. When he released her, she smiled and climbed into the plane.

"Good-bye," said Larry as she started the engine. He backed off as she turned the plane around and took off down the street. She soared into the sky and over Central Park.

Larry felt movement in his pocket as Jed and Octavius poked their heads out.

"There she goes," said Jedediah.

"Straight toward..." said Octavius.

"Canada," Larry finished. Amelia was heading the wrong way. Luckily, she quickly turned around and headed south, back toward the Smithsonian.

Larry hopped up the steps and entered the museum lobby. It was alive with activity. Since Dexter carried the tablet inside, all of the exhibits *just* came to life.

Across the lobby, Dexter handed the tablet to Ahkmenrah. The little monkey chattered humbly.

The young pharaoh smiled. "I forgive you, my simian friend."

The T-rex skeleton nuzzled Larry's side. "Hey, boy," said Larry. He patted the creature's hard skull. "You missed one heck of a night."

Larry strolled past the giant Easter Island head. "What's up, fathead?" he asked. "How was your night?"

"Not as fun, Dum-dum," the head replied in his deep voice.

As Larry moved deeper into the museum, he found Teddy and Sacajawea hugging. The former president gently stroked her face before she left and headed toward the basement. Teddy watched her disappear down the stairs, then turned to Larry. His grin was wider than usual.

"Thank you for bringing them back, Lawrence," he said. "And while I extend to you a hearty well-done, lad, might I point out that they can't hide in the basement forever."

"I know," said Larry. "But I think I have that figured out."

"Sun come, Dum-dum," boomed the Easter Island head.

"Our Moai friend is right," said Teddy. "The dawn will soon be upon us."

Larry walked Teddy back to his horse and display stand. As Teddy climbed back in the saddle, Larry remembered their last meeting. "Hey, Teddy. The other night, you said something about the secret to happiness?"

"Did I?" asked Teddy.

"Yeah, remember? The whole secret to happiness thing?" asked Larry. "You were about to tell me what it was."

"Oh," said Teddy. He glanced around sheepishly. He looked as if he didn't remember.

"It's doing what you love, isn't it?" asked Larry. "With people you love? Right?"

Teddy chuckled. "Actually, I was probably going to say *physical exercise*." He drew his sword and got into position. "But all that stuff's good, too."

Larry laughed and glanced at the museum windows. The sun was just about to rise. He turned back to Teddy. The former president grinned down at him. "Welcome home, son."

A few days later, Larry was back in the museum and back in his night guard uniform. He was busy working the night shift at the Museum of Natural History once more. The only difference was, he wasn't alone. Even though it was nighttime, the museum was full of customers.

As he made his way through the crowd, he passed the information desk. He exchanged a smile with Nick, who sat there doing his homework—just like he used to.

"Well, well, well," said Dr. McPhee. He glanced down at Larry's uniform. "I see the suit still fits, after all these many years."

Larry adjusted his jacket. "It hasn't been that long."

"And what prompted your triumphant return?" asked McPhee. "Not cut out for the corporate jungle after all?"

Larry smiled. "Yeah, I guess not."

McPhee shook his head and gazed at the museum. "Well, clearly the world works in mysterious ways. One day we're getting rid of everything old, the next, some rich, anonymous donor gives us a huge endowment, on the condition that everything stays the same."

"Is that right?" Larry asked, pretending he didn't know about it.

"Yes, well, not *quite* the same," McPhee added. He pointed across the lobby to the Teddy Roosevelt mannequin.

"Bully, lads and ladies!" said Teddy. Very much alive, the former president led a small tour group around the museum. "The name's Theodore Roosevelt. Naturalist, Rough Rider, and twenty-sixth president of these great United States." He ushered the group along. "Come, my friends, the hunt is afoot!"

At the other side of the lobby, Attila the Hun

sat with a group of young children. He excitedly told them a story full of loud yelps and wild hand gestures. Even though he spoke completely in Hun, the kids hung on every word.

Another group of patrons gathered around the Easter Island head. "Welcome, Dum-dums," he boomed. "You bring me gum-gum?"

On the second floor, Ahkmenrah led another tour group. The younger brother of Kahmunrah (and a much nicer pharaoh) appeared to be translating a large wall of hieroglyphics. Dexter stood on a nearby pedestal pointing out each of the pictograms as they went.

Back down below, two teenage boys sat on Rexy's stone platform. They gazed up at the huge dinosaur chewing on a bone.

"This place is lame," said one of the boys. "This thing doesn't even look real."

"Seriously, dude," agreed the other boy. "These animatronics are weak."

Just then, Rexy stood and turned to the boys. His mouth opened wide.

ROOOOOOOOOAAAAAAAR!

The boys' hair blew back and their jaws dropped with wonder. "Whoa," they said.

Watching the entire thing, McPhee shook his head. "Honestly, today's technology is beyond me."

"Yeah," Larry agreed. "It's... something else."

"You! Toddler!" yelled McPhee. He pointed to a little boy giving Sacajawea a hug. "No hugging the displays!" The museum director marched off across the lobby.

Larry was thrilled to be back. Yes, an anonymous donor *did* give a huge amount of money to the museum. The donor had only two conditions for the donation. One: all the old exhibits had to be returned and never again be sent away. And two: the museum had to begin night hours. The donor had to make a pretty big donation to make such demands. Luckily, once Larry sold his company (leaving Ed in charge, of course) he had plenty of money for such a huge donation. Larry didn't mind parting with the company, the prestige, or the money. He was back where he belonged—among his friends.

Larry caught his breath as he spotted a familiar face in the crowd. The woman had long brown hair and wore glasses. And even though she didn't wear a leather flight jacket or a silk scarf, she was the spitting image of Amelia Earhart.

As Larry moved closer, the woman gave him a puzzled look. "Can I help you?" she asked.

Larry realized he had been staring. "Uh, yeah, no...sorry." He cringed with embarrassment. "It's just that you look like someone I know."

"Yeah, I get that a lot," she said with a smile. "I guess I have one of those faces, Mr."—she leaned in to look at his name tag—"Daley."

"It's Larry," he said, extending out a hand. She shook his hand. "I'm Tess."

He couldn't get over how much she looked like Amelia. Larry thought for a moment then decided to ask. "You're not, by any chance, related to Amelia Earhart, are you?"

Tess seemed surprised by the question. "Uh, no," she said. "She was the woman who flew across the Pacific, right?"

"Actually, it was the Atlantic," he corrected. "She was the first woman ever to do it. She was also the first woman to receive the Flying Cross and the first to fly across the forty-eight states."

Tess seemed impressed. "Pretty cool," she said. Larry sighed. "She was."

For a moment, the two simply stared at each other. Then Larry broke the silence. "You know, if you want to see something *really* cool, you should check out the Hall of Miniatures," he suggested. "It can get pretty... *lively* in there."

Tess gave a sly smile. "Really?" She seemed intrigued.

As Larry led her up the steps to the second floor, a toy airplane circled overhead. Riding inside were Jedediah and Octavius. "Heads-up, Gigantor!" shouted Jed as the red plane buzzed by. "Yeeeeeeee-haaaaaah!"

Larry and Tess laughed at the sight—a tiny cowboy and an ancient Roman piloting an airplane. That's what Larry loved about his job. Anything could happen during a night at the museum.

MORE NIGHT AT THE MUSEUM BOOKS FROM BARRON'S

NEW YORK TIMES™ BESTSELLER!

NIGHT AT THE MUSEUM
The Junior Novelization
Leslie Goldman

Night at the Museum was one of the biggest film hits for family audiences of 2006. Now you can relive the movie with this novelized and expanded version of Milan Trenc's picture storybook for children, *The Night at the Museum*. On his very first night at work, the night guard at New York's Museum of Natural History begins to see the museum's exhibits come to life. He tells his son about the many strange things he sees each night. At first reluctant to believe his father's fanciful tales, the son begins to see Dad in a new light when he, too, spends a night at the museum. He discovers that his father's amazing world is real. The film's unusual and entertaining story, starring Ben Stiller, Robin Williams, Mickey Rooney, and Dick Van Dyke, is faithfully recreated in this funny and fanciful novelization for young readers. (Ages 8–12) **Paperback, 128 pp., ISBN 978-0-7641-3576-7**

THE NIGHT AT THE MUSEUM
Milan Trenc

THE ORIGINAL STORYBOOK THAT STARTED IT ALL!

When Larry becomes a night guard at New York's Museum of Natural History, he expects to have an easy job. But on his first night, he dozes off, then wakes up to the most amazing vanishing act in the museum's history. The museum's entire collection of dinosaur skeletons has disappeared! In a panic, Larry rushes from one room to the next—then dashes outside into Central Park, and next door into the planetarium. Where did the skeletons go? Who is the dinosaur thief? —And how in the world can Larry get those dinosaur bones back again? Originally published by Barron's in 1993, this mystery-comedy for kids complements the major motion picture that it inspired. The book features the author's original ~~fun~~ story, with full-color illustrations on every page. (Ages 4–7)

Paperback, 32 pp., ISBN 978-0-7641-3631-3

Please visit **www.barronseduc.com** to view current prices and to order books

BARRON'S

Barron's Educational Series, Inc.
250 Wireless Blvd.
Hauppauge, NY 11788
Order toll-free: 1-800-645-3476
Order by fax: 1-631-434-3723

In Canada:
Georgetown Book Warehouse
34 Armstrong Ave.
Georgetown, Ont. L7G 4R9
Canadian orders: 1-800-247-7160
Fax in Canada: 1-800-887-1594

(#173) R 11/08